THE
THIRTEENTH
GUEST

THE THIRTEENTH GUEST

(or, THE MORGAN MYSTERIES)

ARMITAGE TRAIL

COACHWHIP PUBLICATIONS
Greenville, Ohio

The Thirteenth Guest, by Armitage Trail
© 2022 Coachwhip Publications edition

First published 1929
Armitage Trail, pseudonym for Maurice Coons
    (1902-1930)
CoachwhipBooks.com

ISBN 1-61646-521-2
ISBN-13 978-1-61646-521-6

1

The Girl of the Notes

Gerard Winston read again for the tenth time within five minutes the note which had been the last item of his morning mail:

> *Meet me in the library of the old Morgan home at twelve o'clock tonight. Don't fail!*
> *Marie.*

"Now who in the world is Marie?" growled Winston as he folded the note and dropped it on his paper-littered desk. "And what can she want with me?"

He picked up the note again and examined it closely. The stationery was chaste white of most excellent quality with two intertwined "M's" embossed in dark blue in the upper left-hand corner. The penmanship was of a puritanical style, plain, angular, without flourishes; and with a backward slope indicating stubbornness in the writer. The penmanship of a man or of a very determined woman. But the note was mysterious. It aroused his curiosity in spite of his definite effort to remain unconcerned.

In his work as district attorney of Ricksburg, a progressive little midwestern city, he had received many strange communications, most of them obviously the work of cranks. Some had been foolish and harmless; others had made ridiculous demands; others had recklessly threatened his life. He disregarded them all with a smiling coolness that aroused the admiration of his assistants.

The present note, he decided, was probably just another of the long line that cross the desk of any public official. He dropped the missive into the wastebasket and turned his attention to other matters. But somehow his mind refused to focus this morning. It wavered and wandered but invariably came back to the strange note. He plucked the missive out of the wastebasket angrily and looked at it again. He had but little faith in his diagnosis of its origin. The stationery was dignified. So was the penmanship. And the terse phrasing had a definite, determined ring that was disturbingly businesslike.

The envelope claimed his attention. The paper matched that of the letter. It was perfectly blank except for the address: *Mr. Gerard Winston, Esq., City Hall, City.* He looked at that last word again. City! The letter had been mailed locally. The postmark confirmed this. The letter had gone through the Ricksburg post office at six-thirty the evening before. Which meant nothing. The only clue was the intertwined initials, *M. M.*

One by one, he thought over his somewhat extensive list of feminine acquaintances. Not a Marie among them. Nor one with the initials *M. M.* He spent half an hour going carefully through the *M* division of the local telephone book and city directory. There were several *M. M.'s* but none whose first name was Marie. Which disposed of the writer being a local person unless, of course, he or she was using a false name or the thing was a practical joke.

He considered the latter possibility seriously. It was possible, of course, but not probable. He knew of no one who could wish to perpetrate a practical joke on him. And the stationery argued against such an explanation. A jokester would not go so far as to purchase embossed stationery. He thought of the Morgans themselves. But none of them had lived in the city for years and he had never heard of a Marie in the family anyway.

He went to lunch with the note in his inside coat pocket and his mind in a whirl from the continued but unproductive thought on the matter. Though every line of the note was indelibly imprinted on his memory he read it through three different times during his meal. But it was no plainer on the twentieth reading than on the first.

With the dessert and coffee the waiter brought a small square envelope. The plain superscription: *Mr. Gerard Winston* struck through to the young man's heart like a knife. For the handwriting was the same as in the mysterious note. With trembling fingers he tore open the envelope and extracted a small white card containing three words: *Don't fail. Marie.*

"Where'd you get this?" demanded Winston.

"The head waiter asked me to deliver it to you, sir."

"Ask him to come here immediately."

"Yes, sir."

The head waiter was a plump man with a once-handsome face that showed plainly the ravages of dissipation, and a somewhat condescendingly polite manner that frightened many customers into taking tables they didn't want.

"You gave this note to Schroeder to deliver to me."

"Yes, sir."

"Where'd you get it?"

"A lady gave it to me, sir."

"A lady? What kind of a lady? Describe her."

"She was young, sir; in the early twenties, I should say. A blonde as I remember, dressed in white."

Winston's eyes swept the club dining room. A number of women were present and several in white.

"Is she here now?"

"No, sir. She didn't come into the dining room—just came to the door and handed me the note. She went away at once."

"H'm! You know a lot of people here by sight, don't you?"

"Practically all of the so-called 'smart set,' sir, and a good many that could be called other things."

"Did you recognize this girl?"

"I have never seen her before, sir."

"H'm! Thanks."

Winston looked about nervously as he left the restaurant. It wasn't pleasant to know that one's every move was being followed, even by a woman. This thing was getting serious. Perhaps it was of more importance than he had thought. He considered talking it over with some of his assistants, but feared their ridicule in the face of his casual disposal of other matters of like nature, and remained silent.

He tried to work but his mind was so disturbed that he accomplished but little. At three o'clock he drove out to the country club for a few sets of tennis. Strenuous exercise always cleared his mind. He was a tall young man with a broad-shouldered, lithe figure and a lean, earnest face with piercing gray eyes, a wide forehead whose height was accentuated by bald temples, and a determined mouth. A brilliant future was predicted for him by his friends, and even his enemies—of which he had no lack—admitted that he possessed unusual legal ability.

He reached home shortly after six, healthily tired, his mind rested by the strenuous exercise. Hallud, his colored servant, informed him that dinner would be served within ten minutes, and Winston dashed upstairs for a cold shower and a change of clothes.

The big, old-fashioned home in which he lived alone with the one negro was a part of the comfortable heritage which enabled him to devote his time and talents to public service with no thought of the financial reward involved. Hallud, too, was a part of the estate. He had been in the service of the Winston family since the day of his birth, as had his father before him. His father had been a trusted slave in the service of the older generations of Winstons, who were Virginians. The old slave had proven his religious turn of mind by naming his only son Hallud because it was a Bible name. As he had always explained it to those who asked him about it: "Lawsy, boss, don't you remember wheah it say in de Bible: 'Hallowed be thy name'?"

As Winston adjusted his tie and slipped on the cool light coat he heard the doorbell ring. A vague premonition shot through him and he hurried downstairs. A uniformed boy was mounting a motorcycle in front of the house and Hallud stood in the hallway holding a letter. Winston seized it, then drew in a sharp breath! That unforgettable handwriting! He tore open the envelope with trembling fingers and found a message the exact counterpart of that which had been delivered to him during luncheon: *"Don't fail. Marie,"*

"All right, Marie," he uttered grimly. "I won't."

He saw Hallud staring at him in wide-eyed wonderment, and hastened on to the dining room, slipping the missive into his pocket. He ate in silence, his mind whirling with a hundred doubts, theories, questions. He was thoroughly convinced that the matter was serious and not a joke of some sort. It occurred to him that the whole thing might be a plot on the part of his enemies. A murderer was to go on trial the following week whom Winston had expressed his intention of prosecuting with the utmost vigor. Or the thing might be a "frame up" to get him involved in a compromising situation with some woman so that his political enemies could have something "on him" at the next election. The old Morgan home had been deserted for years. It would be an ideal location for foul play. But he dismissed all these possibilities. He was going and that settled it.

After the meal he settled himself in his comfortable library with a volume of humorous essays and an ancient black pipe. Now that his decision on the matter was definitely made he was strangely quiet. But occasionally his eyes wandered from the book. He found himself thrilled at the prospect of the night's adventure. He wondered whether the thing would turn out to be a matter of consequence or merely a hoax.

He read until eleven-twenty, then shut his book with a snap and rose. The jangling of the telephone halted him just as his foot crossed the threshold into the hall, and he turned back to the instrument on the library table.

"Is this Mr. Gerard Winston?" came a voice in response to his hurried "Hello." It was a soft, cultured feminine voice.

"Yes." His heart was pounding until he could barely hear the sound of his own voice.

"This is Marie, Mr. Winston. The girl of the notes, you know. Don't fail me tonight, *please*. It's a matter of life or death."

He spluttered half a dozen questions into the instrument before he realized that he was talking only to himself. He waited. There was no response. He jiggled the hook and the operator inquired with irritating calm: "Number, please?" He growled an oath and set the instrument back on the table. The girl had hung up.

He hurried upstairs, his face grimly purposeful, and changed into a dark suit. A dark cap and a revolver completed his equipment for the journey. Two minutes later his trim, low-hung roadster swept out of the driveway. As he drove through the business section of the small city he considered stopping at police headquarters and taking an

officer with him. But his pride quickly vetoed such a pro-
posal and he went on alone.

His car sped easily and quickly beyond the business
district, through the residential section and on into the
sparsely settled region beyond. The Morgan home was but
a mile away. He allowed his powerful car to slow down.
It was ten minutes before twelve. He intended to arrive
exactly at the stroke of midnight. There was ample time—
Then one of his tires blew out with a loud explosion. The
left rear one, an examination disclosed. He swore lustily
as he took off his coat and reached for tools. Then a little
twinge of fear caught him under the short ribs. What if
this puncture was a part of the plan?

His keen glance swept his surroundings suspiciously.
The road there descended sharply in conformity with a ra-
vine, then ascended as steeply as it came down. His car was
at the very bottom. Not another headlight showed in any
direction. The road was deserted and on either side were
solid walls of blackness that he knew to be dense woods.
It was an ideal spot for an ambush. He laid his revolver
on the ground beside him as he started to change the tire.

2

The Galloping Corpse

Winston's wrist watch indicated twelve-ten as he came abreast of the Morgan home and slowed abruptly. The tire had proven somewhat troublesome, but he had neither seen nor heard anything further to excite his apprehension. He stopped and for some reason he was thankful that his brakes did not squeak. His eyes narrowed and swept the scene outspread to his right.

The Morgan home was a forbidding object, even in daylight. But seen in the vague funeral blackness of a moonless night it was grim and gruesome, disturbingly suggestive of an ancient prison with a bloody history. It was a huge black bulk set far back from the road. Across the immense breadth of its ground in front were white stone pillars at regular intervals, startlingly distinct against the somber background and awesomely reminiscent of tombstones. In the darkness nothing between them could be seen, but Winston knew that they supported a high rusty iron fence. Further, he knew there were two gates, one in the center giving onto a graveled footpath that led directly to the house; the other a wide one far to the right and giving admittance to a graveled driveway that pursued a tortuous course through the grounds before reaching the house.

At the moment, the house was enveloped in complete darkness. Winston pulled at his collar and took a quick

breath as though something had tried to choke him. He
hesitated an instant. But only for an instant. Then he resolutely reached for the gear lever. He stopped again in
front of the big gate. *It was open!* He stared at the house
with heightened interest. Someone must be within. Never
within his memory had that big gate been open. Whoever
it was must be waiting for *him*—in the darkness.

He shook off with a definite effort the shivery feeling that had started to come over him and drove slowly
through the gateway. He remembered when the Morgan
home and its grounds had been the show place of the entire countryside for miles around. The grounds had been
the especial pride of old Colonel Morgan. He had spent—
it was related by the scandalized natives—more than fifty
thousand dollars to have them beautified with almost
every known tree and shrub. But a dozen years of total
neglect had laid a deathly hand on the once beautiful
place. It was a repellant wilderness now.

The grass had grown to the height of a man's waist
and in many places had even sprouted up unsightly tufts
through the graveled surface of the driveway. Shrubs and
bushes, relieved of the restraint of the pruning knife, had
run amuck. They reached out to each other across the drive
and in spots almost touched. They gave way reluctantly
to Winston's car, brushing against it with harsh, grating
sounds that set his teeth on edge. And more than once a
branch damp with dew laid its clammy embrace upon him.

He stopped under the porte-cochere and climbed out
with deceptive briskness. He wanted to whistle to keep up
his spirits but decided not to. No use letting people know
where you were before you were ready to see them. His
right hand wrapped itself around his revolver with a grasp
positively affectionate, while his left took possession of a
flashlight that was always kept in a door pocket of the car.

He looked up at the house. It was a huge, old-fashioned affair, three stories in height, with a mansard roof pierced with small fancy windows strangely like blind eyes and a semi-circular projection on one side that terminated in a cupola a full story higher than the balance of the building. Not a glimmer of light could be seen.

He literally pushed himself toward the steps, a dark bulk of ten feet to the left His foot struck a small stone and sent it rattling down the path with an alarming racket. In the tense stillness the sound seemed as loud as a machine gun exploding. He stopped and in spite of his resolution considered retreat. Then his jaw set. If the thing were a practical joke he would never hear the last of it if he allowed his nerves to triumph over his nerve. And if it wasn't—well, he had come this far and he intended going the rest of the way. He took a firm hold on himself and ascended the steps. They echoed hollowly under his feet.

He knocked rather weakly, then waited while his heart thumped and his scalp tingled. But nothing happened. He knocked again, louder and longer. Still no response. He left the side entrance rather jauntily and walked around to the front. A heavy, rusty iron knocker decorated the massive weather-beaten front door. He banged it noisily. No response. He banged it again, then waited exactly five minutes by his watch. That was time enough for anyone to reach the door. But no one had. His spirits were the highest they had been since his departure from home. Maybe the whole thing was a joke after all.

But maybe it wasn't. His watch indicated twelve-twenty. He was a third of an hour late. A great deal could happen in that length of time. He tried the door, secretly hopeful that it was securely locked, as it should be. That would end his quest. But it swung open easily, the old, unoiled hinges squeaking eerily. And at that instant he could have

sworn that a tiny flame like a match or candle was suddenly extinguished in the darkness to the rear. He gasped and
explored with his flashlight.

The long cone of yellow light revealed a huge, gloomy
hall with several doors opening off of each side and a
stairway leading upward. The sound of his own breathing
was all that came to his anxious ears. Nothing so scary
there, he decided, and stepped inside. His finger tightened
slightly on the trigger of his revolver as he shot his light
into the first room on the right. It was a stiff, formal parlor with a massive crystal chandelier suspended from the
center of the high ceiling. The furniture was smothered
in white cloth covers. Apparently it contained nothing of
special interest.

He crossed the hall to the first room on the left. A
gasp escaped him. For the long beam of light poking
inquisitively about the room revealed solid shelves of
books. It was the library—the room which was to have
been the scene of the appointment. He advanced a step
across the threshold and began a systematic search of the
room with his torch. The light swept the back wall, then
slowly crept along each side wall. Nothing but shelves of
dusty books, four heavy chairs and a massive table of some
dark wood.

Winston noticed with a start that the furniture there
was not covered. The room must have been occupied recently. Then he jumped and almost yelled as the beam
of light, wandering about the floor, centered on a startling object. It was the inert body of a woman, stretched
out carefully on the dusty carpet. She was young and well
formed. He could see plainly the outline of her supple,
rounded limbs and body through the loose, sunken folds
of the thin white dress. He started again as he noticed that
she was a blonde and dressed entirely in white.

He forced himself to approach closer and make a cursory examination. She was dead. Finger marks on her throat and the swollen blackness of her once-lovely young face indicated that she had been choked to death. Was this the mysterious Marie? He wondered. Her appearance tallied exactly with the description of the girl who had sent the note in to him at luncheon and she looked like a girl who would have the sort of voice he had heard so recently in a final plea for him not to fail. If this was Marie, who had killed her and why? And had his tardiness for their appointment been the cause of her death? He felt a little guilty about it. This thing was far from the practical joke he had suspected.

A careful search of the room revealed three clues: a dainty handkerchief with the initial *"M"* in one corner, a small white and pink carnation badly rumpled and without a stem, and an extremely thin, all-metal pocketknife of distinctive appearance. The handkerchief seemed to corroborate his deduction of the girl's identity. He could make nothing of the other two articles—yet. Absently he shoved all three into his coat pocket.

There was a telephone on the table and he went to it without expectation that it was connected. But in a moment came a cool, impersonal "Number, please." He gave one and made a mental note to talk to the manager of the telephone company the next morning.

"Hello, police headquarters?" he said at last. "Is Detective Grump in? I'd like to speak to him, please. . . . Hello . . . Grump? This is Gerard Winston. Got anything special to do for the next couple of hours? No? Then I wish you'd do something for me. I've got a classy mystery on hand that must be unraveled. From all appearances it'll be a whopper. Yeah, murder. Don't say a word to anybody but come to the old Morgan home at once. Yes, the old

Morgan home. I'm there now. I'll be waiting for you. Yes, alone. No, I've got a gun. Don't ask me any questions now. I'll tell you everything when you get here. And it'll make your eyes stick out. Remember, not a word to anybody and step on it."

He frowned as he looked at the body again under the light of his electric torch. Poor girl! What sort of business had she been mixed up in that had turned out so seriously it had taken her life? She did not have the appearance of a girl who would be found on the wrong side of the law. But somehow he could not reconcile her with the determined handwriting in the notes.

One thing certain, this affair was far from a joke. It was a stark tragedy. He wondered with a sudden involuntary little shiver if it would stop with the death of the beautiful girl who had so wanted to see him. A hundred questions leaped from the depths of his active brain and hammered relentlessly at his reason. But he had no means of answering them. He shook his head fiercely to clear it and looked around the room. The walls seemed to be solid. The two windows were tightly closed and locked. The heavy layer of dust along their frames and on the locks had not been disturbed. The murderer—for the girl unquestionably had been murdered—must have entered and departed through the door which had been the means of his own entrance.

With a start he remembered the light he believed he had seen at the end of the long hall when the heavy front door swung open under his touch. But no! he must have been mistaken. His heightened senses had played him a trick. But had they? It was possible that the murderer had been alarmed by his knocking but had not been able to escape before his entrance. He recalled the warmth of the girl's body at the moment of his first examination. He stooped now and forced himself to touch gently one of the slender white hands. Not yet had the dread coldness of death settled down on the lovely form.

In a sudden accession of anger at the unknown criminal he rushed out into the hall. The man—it must be a man, for a woman would hardly have the strength to strangle another to death—might still be in the house. His light darting here and there, its inquisitive beam poking into unexpected corners, investigating vague shapes that made his heart pound a bit before it revealed their true innocence, he went from room to room. All were much like the first—large apartments with high ceilings, musty, stifling air and massive furniture carefully clothed in white covers like shrouds deathly grayish with dust. He realized in passing that the place must be a veritable treasure-house of antiques.

As he reached the end of the hall a clean, cool current of air made him pause. Something was open in the rear. With an effort he held command of his nerves and went on through the dining room into the kitchen with its old-fashioned wood-burning cook stove and enormous white cupboards on every side. The back door was open, admitting the gusty night breeze. He looked out but the beam of his light could not penetrate the dense, jungle-like undergrowth.

He closed the door. The kitchen seemed to offer nothing of interest and he went back to the dining room. He noticed with suddenly aroused interest that the furniture there was not covered. Strange! All over the house every article was done up as carefully as though it would fall to pieces if exposed. But here not a single cover could be seen. Such a condition was more than a coincidence. It might be an important clue.

A scream rang out somewhere in the house. It was a high-pitched, piercing, feminine scream and it shattered the tense silence like an explosion. A chilly, unpleasant sensation shot up Winston's spine and tingled at the base of his brain. He hoped the sound would ring out again if only to prove that it was not a product of his imagination and heightened senses in the weird surroundings. It didn't, but he heard running footsteps.

He dashed out into the hall, his revolver ready for instant use, his searchlight flashing in all directions. The running footsteps rang out loudly. They seemed to be ascending stairs. He came abreast of the stairway and shot his light upward. Then he stood still, barely repressing a yell, while his heart and brain seemed to freeze within him of horror. *For the girl whom he had left stretched out dead on the floor of the library was running upstairs.*

3

The Face at the Window

The girl turned as the light struck her and looked back, her face contorted with an expression of stark terror. Then she seemed to leap upward twice as fast as before. Winston stood at the foot of the stairs for what seemed like eternity, unable to move, unable to breathe, unable to think. The blood-congealing awfulness of the supernatural spectacle he was witnessing held him spellbound.

Then his common sense came to the fore. He didn't believe in ghosts. His jaw set as he made his resolution and with a tremendous explosion of will power he leaped up the carpeted steps after the running girl of whose death he had been positive.

He held the beam steadily on the girl until she reached the head of the stairs, Then she turned to the left and he lost her. Three at a time he ascended the long flight of steps, his feet pounding dust from the old carpet. At the top, he followed to the left. But the girl had vanished. The hall was empty. He peered into every room on the second floor. He found nothing but heavy furniture carefully wrapped in its white shrouds.

The stairway leading to the third floor was to the right of that which he had ascended. The girl had turned to the left. She had not gone up. But she had vanished on the second floor. He went back downstairs, firmly resolved to search every nook and corner of the house when Detective Grump arrived. Two could do a more thorough job than one. And there were a lot of things about this old house which needed investigating.

He paused at the door of the library, shooting his light inside. And received his second paralyzing shock of the past quarter of an hour. The girl's body lay exactly as he had first found it, stretched out flat on the floor, face up, with the hands extended parallel at the sides. He walked over and peered down at it in wonderment. Then he forced himself to make another examination. His exploring fingers, could find no trace of respiration or pulse. The girl was dead!

He shot his light around the room. Nothing was disturbed. He retreated to the hall rather hurriedly. Such a gruesome situation was beyond his powers of deduction. He had figured out some intricate problems during his legal career, but a dead woman running up and down stairs was a little too much.

Winston looked at his watch. Five minutes of one. He had been in this weird house but thirty-five minutes. It seemed like as many years. He frowned. Detective Grump should have arrived. And so should he, twenty minutes before he had. Accidents could happen. He looked back into the dark library rather guiltily. Well, he couldn't sit and hold his hands until the officer arrived. He went back to the dining room.

The Morgan dining room was worthy of attention, even under ordinary circumstances. It was large, easily twenty-five feet square, and with the high ceiling common to the rest of the house. A splendid-crystal chandelier with innumerable swaying pendants that clanked together at times hung from the exact center of the ceiling. The fixtures were fitted for candles and Winston saw that a number of them were still in place. He clambered up on a chair and lighted them, then emitted a breath of relief as they flared up, bathing everything in the soft yellow glow. He could see the room in its entirety now, and its old-fashioned splendor aroused his admiration. The large expanse of floor was almost entirely covered by an Oriental rug whose fine quality was obvious even after so many years of inattention. The furniture was square and massive, of solid walnut or mahogany, blackened with age. The seats and backs of the chairs were of leather, scuffed with use and mouldy from neglect. Splendid hangings, now dusty and moth-eaten, were at the windows, and four oil paintings of evident worth decorated the walls.

But the most striking point about the room was the table. It was set for dinner. Dishes, silver, stemmed goblets, everything was in place for a perfectly appointed meal. Winston counted the covers. *Thirteen!* He wondered with a little shiver if there was anything about the old house that was not weird or that had no sinister significance. The genteel dimness of the room did not permit of close examination of things and he flashed his electric torch over the table. Every article there was covered with a thick layer of dust. Months or perhaps years had elapsed since that table had been set for dinner with the evil number of thirteen guests. What had happened to prevent its occurrence?

Winston turned his attention to the huge sideboard that covered more than half the space of one wall. At either end were two glass candlesticks containing green candles and in the center a tarnished silver tray containing a cut glass decanter and glasses. The decanter was better than a third full. He removed the stopper and the smell of choice Scotch whiskey tantalized his nostrils.

"Whoever ordered that knew what he was about," he surmised and replaced the stopper. The stuff might be poisoned. Considering the other things in the house he was positive it must be.

He cast a keen glance into the glasses one by one. And he found two with a few drops of brownish liquid in their depths and the same odor that the decanter contained. Two people had secured a drink from that decanter within the past hour or two.

Near the tray rested a small silver plate containing a quantity of ashes and more than a dozen cigarette stubs. No dust showed on them. He lifted one to his nose. The odor was strong and fresh. They had been smoked during the evening. He examined them closely. They were of two kinds; the slender brown paper type filled with strong cigar tobacco that is found almost exclusively in Havana and other tropical cities, and a high-class Turkish blend with cork tips.

"Interesting combination," he murmured.

A thunderous knocking on the front door startled him into tense expectancy. Then he laughed nervously and hurried out into the hall. It was Grump, of course. But why didn't he come on in? The door wasn't locked. Perhaps he preferred company when entering a place with the air and reputation of the old Morgan home. Winston chuckled to himself and reached for the knob. He almost pulled his arm from its socket.

The door was locked.

Quickly he turned the key and Grump came in, a heavy but alert man with thin lips, a resolute jaw, a sharp nose and sharper eyes. The suspense of the unknown will shake the courage of even the bravest man. The detective was scared and he showed it. His face was slightly pale; his hat pushed back and his forehead beaded with great drops of perspiration. His right hand was clenched about the butt of a large police revolver.

"This is a hell of a place to throw a party at night," he exploded. "Where'd you get the hooch? Musta been strong stuff."

"Come in and make yourself at home, Grump," invited Winston cheerily. "Charming evening and a lovely old home to spend it in. There's whiskey and cigars in the dining room."

"I wouldn't mind a drink just now. Where is the dining room?"

"Nothing doing, Grump. We'll both need a clear head to unravel this thing. There's been a mysterious murder here tonight."

"Well, how'd you get in on it?"

Winston gave the detective a concise account of the events since his receipt of that first strange note in his morning mail. When he finished, Grump laughed shortly.

"Sounds like a pipe dream," he grunted. "Let's take a look at this dame."

In grim triumph Winston led the way into the library and turned his flashlight on the body—or rather where the body had been. *It was gone!* Anxiously he swung the light about until its beam had covered every foot of the floor. There was no trace of the body.

"Good God!" he exclaimed hoarsely. "That body was here ten minutes ago."

"Perhaps she's gone out to take a walk around the block," suggested Grump, grimly sarcastic. "First she runs up and down stairs and now she vanishes altogether. And dead all the time. She's one of the liveliest 'stiffs' I ever heard of. . . . Listen, Winston, you're a friend of mine and I think a lot of you. But you're either drunk tonight or you're losin' your mind. Come on, I'll take you home and—"

"You'll *not* take me home," snapped Winston furiously. "You know I don't drink and my mind is as clear as it ever was. Every word I've told you is the absolute truth. I can prove quite a bit of it. In fact, the disappearance of this body is only additional proof that the whole matter is a deep mystery with far-reaching consequences."

"H'm! Let's see the proof!"

In rapid succession the young district attorney exhibit-ed the three strange notes he had received from the nebu-lous Marie, the handkerchief, carnation and knife he had found near the body in the library. Then he escorted the detective back to the dining room and showed him the various clues there.

"Now what do you think?" demanded Winston.

"There's something to it," admitted Grump. "Looks like it might be an interesting case."

They made an exhaustive search of the dining room. In the sideboard they found an extensive stock of liquor, the bottles covered with dust. But one bottle of Scotch whiskey showed positive traces of having been handled recently. Sev-eral plain fingerprints were visible. They might lead to some-thing. Then the 'phone rang. The metallic jangling breaking the tense silence startled them both speechless for a moment.

"Who could be calling here?" asked Grump a trifle breathlessly.

"Lord knows. Did you mention this at headquarters?"

"Not a word to anybody. Did you tell—"

"Nobody but you knows where I am tonight."

The instrument was still ringing insistently. They hur-ried into the library and Winston answered.

"Hello, Thornton?" said a strange voice quickly. It was a deep, commanding voice with an undercurrent of anger.

"Yes," answered the district attorney. He might secure some valuable information.

"You're a damned liar," snapped the other.

With a sudden click the line went dead. Winston jig-gled the hook frantically while Grump looked on in won-derment.

"*Hello! . . . Hello! . . . Hello!* Operator! This is District Attorney Winston speaking. Trace that call, please. Yes, he just hung up. Quickly, please."

"A stranger calling somebody named Thornton," he explained to the detective as he impatiently awaited the operator's report. "Thornton . . . Thornton . . . I wonder who he is. He was expected to be here anyhow. Must be one of the two who drank whiskey in the dining room tonight."

The telephone jangled again and he leaped at it like a terrier at a rat. When he turned back to Grump disappointment was evident in his face.

"The call came from one of the public booths at the Hotel St. Giles. No way of running down anything there. I wonder who that fellow was. Sounded as if he was mad about something."

His voice trailed off into silence as he saw the imperturbable Grump stiffen like a hunting dog who has caught the scent. The detective's jaw dropped. His eyes widened to their uttermost limits and seemed to strain outward as if trying to escape from their sockets. He tried to speak but the words wouldn't come, and he pointed hesitantly with an arm that trembled as though afflicted with palsy.

Winston's heart pounded as he turned to look where his companion pointed. Then it seemed to stop altogether and he felt the cold perspiration break out suddenly all over him. *Framed in one of the library windows was the face of the girl Winston had seen dead on the floor of that very room.* Nothing was visible below or around it. Expressionless, swaying a little from side to side, it seemed to float in thin air.

4

Dead Again

While the two men stared in open-mouthed amazement the face grew fainter and fainter until it disappeared entirely. Grump sighed heavily and mopped his forehead.

"I don't believe in ghosts," he said breathlessly. "But I never saw anything like that."

"Perhaps you'll admit now that I was neither drunk nor crazy."

"Rather. As long as we've known each other I shouldn't have doubted your word for a moment. But your story *did* sound fishy—"

"I know. The whole thing is mighty queer."

"Worse than that. There's something deep behind all this. And I purpose that we find out what it is. There's some secret to this old house." He looked at his watch. "It's after two now. We can't get enough light to do much tonight. Let's go back to town and have some sleep, then come out in the morning."

"Suits me. But something important might happen out here while we are gone."

"I'll 'phone headquarters for a coupla men to come out and keep an eye on things." He reached the telephone and gave a number. "Hello, police headquarters? MacGill? . . . Grump. I'm out at the old Morgan home on the Lakeview road. District Attorney Winston called me out here on a case. Yeah. He's here with me now. There's been some queer doin's here tonight. We're comin' back to town but we don't want to leave the house unguarded. Send out a coupla men to keep an eye on things. No, just ordinary harness bulls. Tell 'em to step on it, too. . . What? You don't say?" There was quickened interest in his voice and he glanced at Winston meaningly. "Give me the description . . . Thanks."

"What is it?" queried the other anxiously as the detective set the instrument down on the table.

"MacGill says the body of a girl was found on Twenty-third street about a half an hour ago. In the early twenties, 'bout five feet seven, weight maybe a hundred and twenty-five, a good-lookin' blonde, well dressed all in white, evidently been choked to death."

"That's the exact description of the girl I found dead in this very room," said Winston excitedly. "What did they do with her?"

"Hauled her over to Osterman's undertaking parlor."

"We must see that body the minute we get to town. I wonder how it disappeared from here."

"That is a mystery. But it is no bigger puzzle than that face at the window and all the other queer things that have happened here tonight. I haven't seen near as much as you have but I've seen enough to convince me that somep'n' mighty funny's goin' on around here."

They walked out on the large front porch to await the coming of the Ricksburg officers. The moon was descending in the west. Under the silvery light the tangled wilderness of the Morgan grounds took on the unearthly appearance of the setting for an ominous fairy tale.

"Creepy old place, ain't it?" said Grump.

"Yes. It always was. Even before it was deserted after the death of old Colonel Morgan. The Morgans were a queer family. Nobody ever knew much about 'em.

"Made their money in mining in the west, didn't they?"

"So I've understood. They must have had plenty of it, the way they lived. But they never had anything to do with local people. I'll bet there aren't five people in the city of Ricksburg today who ever saw the inside of this house."

"And I'll bet there aren't five who want to."

"Perhaps not. A lot of grim legends have grown up around it."

"With all the money they must have had it seems like they would have lived in a big city like New York or Chicago. Why did they settle here?"

"They never told and nobody was able to find out."

"English, weren't they?"

"So it's said."

"Did the old man die a natural death?"

"Some say he did. Others say he didn't. I don't know. My uncle was the Morgan family doctor. He was a little suspicious about the old colonel's death, but the family insisted it was paralysis—that the then old man had had two slight strokes years before—so my uncle made no effort to have an investigation instituted. In after years he often wished he had. It troubled his conscience quite a bit."

"Did anyone have a motive for murdering Morgan?"

"Not that anybody knew of. But it was rather strange that the rest of the family deserted the house immediately and not one of them have ever been heard of since."

"Who got the money?" asked Grump suspiciously with the acumen of the detective.

"I never heard."

"What did the family consist of?"

"The old colonel, his wife, a son and a daughter."

"A daughter! How old was she?"

"About nine or ten when her father died."

"That would make her twenty-one or two now?"

"Yes." Winston was beginning to see where the detective's questions were leading and he mentally kicked himself that he hadn't thought of the same thing.

"What was her name?"

"I don't remember. She never mixed with the other children in town. Had a governess so she didn't go to the public school. I only saw her once."

"Do you remember what she looked like?"

"Yes. She was a beautiful child with long golden curls."

"Golden curls? A blonde? About twenty-one or two years old. Remember the monogram on the stationery used for those strange notes? Two intertwined 'M's, I'll bet a month's pay that the mysterious girl who wrote you those notes and whom you found here tonight was Marie *Morgan*."

A long silence followed the detective's excited declaration.

"It's possible you're right, Grump," admitted the district attorney at last. "I must say your deductions are logical. But what could bring her back here under such strange circumstances?"

"That's what we must find out."

"Seems to me there's a lot of things we must find out. I wonder if we can."

"Of course we can. There never was a mystery that couldn't be unraveled."

"A good many aren't solved."

"I know it. But it's because they aren't run down like they should be."

The district attorney felt his arm seized suddenly in a vise-like grip.

"What's that?" came a low, tense growl from Grump.

His right hand pointed down toward the road and Winston's eyes followed it. A light was moving among the dense undergrowth.

"Can't see it plain enough to be sure what it is," answered Winston. "But it's too real to be supernatural. Seems to be coming closer."

"It is. Let's get behind these posts and see what happens."

Each stepped behind one of the wooden posts supporting the heavy roof that projected out over the wide porch, their figures completely hidden by the shadow. Winston saw Grump draw his revolver, then their eyes riveted anxiously to the advancing light.

The glow seemed too powerful to be that of a lantern. It appeared to be about four feet above the ground and wavered considerably. Reaching the edge of the bushes it shot toward the house long enough for the men hidden there to discern that it was a flashlight. Then it snapped off suddenly and a dark figure approached the building.

"Somebody's coming," whispered Winston hoarsely. "Don't say anything until he gets as close as he'll come."

The strange figure came on slowly but steadily until the hidden men could see it was a tall, well-built man wearing a cap with a long motoring coat over his clothes. He hesitated several moments at the bottom of the steps, as though trying to see or hear something suspicious, then ascended quickly. Grump leaped out of concealment, his gun plainly visible. The stranger jumped and his right hand leaped for the side pocket of his coat.

"Keep your hands in sight," snapped Grump sternly, an ugly edge to his voice. "We're not hold-up men and we won't hurt you. We merely want to ask you a few questions."

The stranger stared fascinated at the round black muzzle pointed unwaveringly toward his wishbone and shivered a little. Then his right hand slid away empty from his coat pocket and he stood blinking in the sudden glow of Winston's flashlight thrown full in his face. He was a rather good-looking young man about thirty years of age with a lean, tanned face, a small, carefully trimmed dark mustache and keen dark eyes.

"What's the idea?" he demanded. "I'm not accustomed to being treated in this way."

"Are you accustomed to walking about the grounds of a deserted house at two in the morning?" retorted Grump sarcastically.

"What is it to you?" It was evident that the young man wasn't in the least cowed by the unexpected encounter.

"I'm Detective Grump of Ricksburg," snapped the officer and exhibited his badge. "And this is—"

"Never mind who I am," commanded Winston. He was keeping his face out of the light. He didn't care to have his connection with the case known publicly just yet.

"Who are you and what are you doing here?" demanded Grump.

"I'm Doctor Sherwood of Chicago. I have a brother living here and have been visiting him the past week. We're both interested in spiritualism and he's told me quite a bit about this old place. Some friends were over from Centerville to see us tonight and I drove them home. Coming back a few minutes ago I saw lights in this house. I knew the place had been deserted for years so I stopped in the hope of seeing some psychic phenomena."

"Humph! A very pretty story," sneered Grump. Always a good remark when one could think of no questions which would be likely to break down a recital which didn't coincide with one's own theories.

"Well, it's true," returned the young man spiritedly. "Believe it or not as you please. I've done nothing wrong and I have nothing to hide. . . . May I ask what the police are doing here at this time of the morning?"

"You may not!" snapped Grump. "But it's on official business, you may be sure."

"I wonder," said the young man calmly.

"Wonder what?" demanded the detective angrily.

"If it's on official business," answered the stranger coolly. There was a humorous lilt in his voice and the corners of his mouth twitched as though he wanted to laugh.

Grump growled and tossed his head like a dog faced by a much smaller but untested adversary. Doctor Sherwood smiled disarmingly.

"Now that I've found the lights here are of human origin I have no further interest in the place. I presume you'll have no objections to offer to my departure."

"Not so fast, young fellow, not so fast," commanded Grump loftily. He could think of no questions he wanted to ask the stranger, but he hated to see anyone slip through his fingers unscathed.

"Where does your brother live?" asked Winston, speaking in a very deep tone in an attempt to disguise his voice.

"Six-fourteen East Twenty-third street."

"Oh! Has he a 'phone?"

"Yes. Eastlake seven-eight-three-one."

"H'm! Just a moment!" Winston disappeared inside the house.

5

The Body Found

"Who is that man?" demanded Doctor Sherwood.

"Somebody you'd better not fool with," answered Grump darkly.

"Why should I want to fool with him?"

"That's what we're going to find out," snapped the detective with a triumphant grin. And the worried expression that crossed the young man's face caused tremendous satisfaction to well up within him.

Winston hurried out.

"You can go now, Doctor Sherwood," he said pleasantly, "on one condition—that you won't leave Ricksburg without permission from the district attorney's office."

"I won't promise any such thing," exploded the young man. "It's an outrage! I've done nothing wrong—"

"Of course, you haven't, doctor," answered the district attorney calmly. "And if you'll promise to keep it confidential I'll let you in on a little inside information that will make you see the thing in a different light."

"Very well. I promise."

Winston disregarded Grump's warning poke in the ribs.

"Some very strange things have occurred here tonight. We don't know all about them ourselves yet and we may need the testimony of every one who has been near the place tonight. So you see why I'm making this request."

"Oh, well, in that case I'll give you my word on the matter."

"Thank you. We don't want to cause you any inconvenience whatsoever but merely get your co-operation, so whenever you wish to leave for your home call at the district attorney's office. You'll find him easy to reason with. He'll no doubt take your signed deposition at once on any points that you may know about and you will be free to go immediately. You see," he added half-apologetically, "a witness often thinks he knows nothing of value. Alone, his information would not be worth anything. But taken in conjunction with the testimony of other witnesses and made a part of the chain it helps to build up a conclusive case."

"I see. I'll be glad to give you any assistance I can and you have my promise on the matter of my departure."

He turned and started down the steps.

"Go with him," commanded Winston in a whisper. "Look his car over carefully and get the license number."

The detective plunged down the steps in pursuit. Doctor Sherwood looked up, annoyed.

"There's a path to the right here," said Grump in an attempt to account for his presence. "I'll show you the way."

The two figures disappeared in the shadow of the trees and bushes. Winston, waiting on the porch, heard an automobile whirr into life, then a car rushed away. Almost immediately there was a rustling through the undergrowth, and Grump appeared in the open, hurrying toward the house.

"It's an Illinois license, all right," admitted the detective and passed over a slip of paper. "There's the number. He's got a Chicago city license, too. Seems like that much of his story is correct."

"The rest of it seems to be, too. When I went in the house before I released him, I telephoned the number he had given me. The man who answered volunteered the information that it was the Sherwood home before I revealed what I wanted. He identified this man positively as his brother. That's the reason I released the fellow."

"But do you believe his story about spiritualism and so forth?"

"I don't know. Looking at it one way, it sounds all right. Looking at it another, it doesn't. I'm going to find out the truth. We'll investigate him thoroughly later on."

The conversation died abruptly as they heard the sound of an approaching automobile. Then two long cones of light shone through the undergrowth and the engine growled in discontent as the car came up the drive in the second speed. Winston and Grump reached the end of the porch as the car stopped under the porte-cochere. Two uniformed men climbed out glancing about nervously.

"Right this way, boys," called Grump, maliciously mischievous. "The ghost convention is in session and awaiting you."

Startled by the sound of Grump's voice the two uniformed men jumped, then laughed shakily.

"So it's you, is it, you blithering idiot?" demanded one as he reached the porch and made a playful pass at Grump with an enormous fist that would have been sufficient to fell an ox. "What sort of a party is this you're puttin' on out here in the woods?"

"A mighty interesting one, Murphy," answered the detective seriously. The darkness hid the grimly humorous twinkle in his eyes. "Mr. Winston came out here tonight to meet a lady who asked him to. When he got here he found her in the library as dead as a door nail. While he was lookin' through the house he heard a yell and saw her runnin' upstairs. He followed and she vanished right before his eyes. When he come back down, there she lay in the library just as he'd left her when he started his search."

"For the love of God!" exclaimed the big Irishman piously.

"Mr. Winston went on with his search then after 'phonin' to headquarters for me. When I got here we went in the library, and there wasn't a sign of the body. And when I 'phoned headquarters for two men to come here MacGill told me the body had been found over on Twenty-third street. It's been taken to Osterman's, but of course they can't keep the poor girl's spirit caged up."

A gasp rattled in Murphy's throat and he looked about fearsomely. His smaller companion laughed shortly.

"Ah, Grump," he exclaimed disbelievingly. "You and, your stories. Sometimes you can almost make a person believe what you're sayin'. You should be a politician the way you can lie."

"Every word of that is the positive truth, men," affirmed Winston seriously. "This is an important murder case you're in on. You're to stay here until relieved, keep your eyes open *all the time,* let nobody enter the house and report to headquarters the moment anything suspicious occurs."

"Yes, sir, we'll do that all right with ghosts and everything runnin' loose," promised Murphy heavily.

"If you go to sleep you'll very likely never wake up again," shouted Grump maliciously from his seat in Winston's roadster as the young man began backing down the driveway.

Their first stop was at police headquarters, and Lieutenant MacGill at the desk listened respectfully while District Attorney Winston gave him a concise account of the night's happenings.

"Please keep this confidential," requested Winston when he had finished. "Above all things, don't let the newspapermen get hold of it. I believe this is an important case and premature publicity might wreck everything.

In fact, it probably would. So keep it all under your hat except the finding of the girl's body. Let the newspapers have that. We want the girl identified if possible and the sooner the better. But don't give them any details. Grump and I are going to Osterman's now to see this body. And I want a man to go along with us to leave there as a guard if we find it is the body we think it is. If any calls come from the men at the Morgan place relay them on to me at home immediately no matter what time it is."

Winston and Grump piled into the rakish roadster again and a uniformed officer took his place in the rumble seat behind.

Ricksburg possessed no regular morgue, the embalming room at Osterman's undertaking establishment serving the purpose nicely, for the occasions when a morgue was needed were few and far between in that peaceful little city. Except for Osterman's assistant the place was deserted when Winston and his companions arrived. And when Winston presented his card they were led into the embalming room at once.

"That's it," affirmed the district attorney the moment his eyes rested on the still figure stretched out on a lounge-like affair in the center of the room.

It was Grump's first view of the body and he spent several minutes in a thorough examination. Winston lighted a cigarette and stared at the rows of bottles with skull-and-crossbones labels which filled two shelves that extended the entire length of the small room.

"Choked to death, all right," said the detective at last. "Not a wound on the body. Been dead several hours. Well, we'd better get some sleep. We've got a busy day ahead of us tomorrow."

"Rather!" Winston turned to the policeman. "Stay here in this very room until you are relieved. Considering what has already happened an attempt may be made to kidnap this body. Guard it with your life. Shoot if necessary. 'Phone me at once if anything happens."

It was after three o'clock when Winston slipped on a dressing-gown over his pajamas, lighted a pipe and sat down to think over the day's events. There were many things about this strange case that he was utterly unable to understand. Most important of these was his own connection with it. Just where did he fit into the jigsaw puzzle? Why had that mysterious girl who seemed dead one moment and alive the next called him into the affair? He was positive that he had never seen her before. He had never even heard of her. Why had she been so insistent on his presence in the Morgan library at midnight? And had his tardiness been the cause of her death? Had his lateness completely altered the course of the mysterious affair?

6

The Mysterious Caller

Winston rose at eight the following morning and dressed rather listlessly. He felt fagged out. His sleep had been fitful and unsatisfactory, disturbed by unpleasant dreams and startling visions of vague, uncanny terrors about to leap upon him. He wondered if they were prophetic, then laughed harshly at his own fears and went down to breakfast.

With an anxiety he could not have explained he seized the morning paper. A glaring headline on the front page struck his eye: *"Unknown girl dies mysteriously."* Sensations in Ricksburg were scarce. They had made the most of this one. The column-long article beneath the headline had evidently been written by a reporter with a vivid imagination and he had used it all. He offered half a dozen possibilities for the strange occurrence, none of which were anywhere near the truth as Winston knew it to be.

The district attorney wasn't surprised. The truth of the matter was so uncannily bizarre, so far beyond the bounds of reason, that nobody could be expected to believe it when it was told to them, much less imagine it. It was evident that MacGill had obeyed orders. The article covered nothing except the finding of the body, but stressed the placing of a police guard over it, and hinted darkly at some deep mystery behind the whole thing. Winston chuckled at that. If they only knew the truth—

He reached his office on the second floor of the city hall shortly after nine o'clock and found reporters from both the morning and evening papers awaiting him. Henry Robinson of the evening *Clarion* was a slight, meek man of thirty with a thin face freckled in spots, sparse sandy hair of no determinable color and watery blue eyes hidden deeply behind shell-rimmed glasses with abnormally thick lenses. But he was a successful news gatherer despite his insignificant appearance, and he never wrote anything unless he knew it to be true.

In direct contrast to him was Dodge of the morning *Beacon,* a burly, red-faced fellow of twenty-seven who affected checked suits and derby hats and appraised good-looking women with unbearable effrontery, then winked gloatingly to whoever happened to be with him. He wanted to be known as a "hard-boiled" police reporter and boasted that there wasn't a "tough egg nor a rotten joint in town" that he didn't know. There were none who disputed that.

"Well, look who's here?" he exclaimed with unwarranted familiarity as Winston appeared. "Like to have a little session with you, chief."

"What about?" asked the district attorney blandly as he strode into his private office and hung up his hat, the two reporters at his heels.

"Why, this mysterious murder last night. That girl. The good-lookin' blonde, you know. Didn't you read the article about it in our sheet this morning?"

"Oh, *that?* Yes, I did. Rather neatly gotten up. Sounded like your style."

Dodge grinned and took the bait.

"It was. Dashed it off early this morning just after I found out about the thing from MacGill. Little Romeo here was still in bed. But the early bird gets the worm."

He ignored the fact that Robinson served an afternoon paper and the information would not have been of the slightest value to him in the middle of the night.

"But what do you want to talk to me about that for? Why should I be expected to know anything about it?" pursued Winston, anxious to see if his connection with the mystery had been discovered.

"You have the inside track of all criminal news, of course, Mr. Winston," answered Robinson mildly. "I thought you might be able to give me a little something new so we could carry a different story than the *Beacon* had this morning."

Winston believed Robinson's explanation though he only heard it subconsciously. His attention was centered on Dodge. He didn't exactly like the sly look in that gentleman's eyes. His even glance bored straight into the burly reporter and he waited until the silence became painful.

"I thought the scandal sheet might try somep'n' like that, so I hopped around to see that they didn't get anything I wasn't in on."

"Which was entirely unnecessary," retorted Winston sharply. "You know I never discriminate. Any news I may have is given to both papers at the same time. Regarding this affair, I have nothing to say at the present time. The matter hasn't been brought to my attention—er—officially as yet. When it is, I shall, of course, institute an investigation. If I discover anything of importance or of interest to the general public I shall telephone both papers at the same time and request them to send around a man to hear what I have to say. And as you know, I prefer that both reporters be present together."

The two reporters turned to go and Winston sat down at his desk. Dodge paused at the door.

"I'll be back later on—Maybe you'll think of something to say."

The door closed behind the newspapermen.

Winston looked up quickly, a puzzled, angry expression on his face. What had the fellow meant? His tone had been threatening. Winston's jaw set and he half rose with the intention of calling Dodge back and having a show-down immediately. Then he sat down again and lighted a cigar before plunging into his mail. His time was too valuable to quarrel with an impudent reporter.

Winston went through his mail quickly, hopeful that it would contain another startling note which might help to clarify the amazing situation in which he found himself involved as a result of the note he had received the morning before. At the same time he was a little fearful of what he might find, vaguely afraid that among his mail might be something which would involve him deeper in the web of mysterious circumstances.

But the return cards in the corners of the envelopes indicated their prosaic origin. He opened none of them. There was a light knock on the door and Detective Grump came in.

"Seen the article in the *Beacon* this morning?" he asked abruptly.

"Yes. It was one of Dodge's. He was here a few minutes ago trying to get some more information."

"He caught me at headquarters just now. Asked me a lot of questions that I refused to answer. Told him I didn't know a thing about the affair. He grinned in a way I didn't like at all."

"He did the same thing here. Said he'd come back to see me later in the day—that I might think of something to say by that time. His tone was threatening. I wonder what he knows."

"You never can tell. He's a sly one and crooked as a dog's hind leg. But I guess we can take care of him all right. He may be hard-boiled but he's no harder than some other folks I know," added the detective meaningly.

"Let's go down to the morgue," proposed Winston, "and see if the body has been identified yet."

"Suits me," assented Grump. "I think I'll stay around there awhile today and watch the people that go through. Might pick up a valuable clue from the expression of some-body's face as they look at the body."

"That's possible," agreed Winston. "I have several things to do this morning. Call me up at the office about eleven and we'll make plans for the rest of the day."

They made a quick trip to Osterman's undertaking es-tablishment. Already a crowd of morbidly curious people, attracted by the sensational article in the morning paper, was assembled outside. A few men and children, but most-ly women, they forced their way inside the building in typical gate-crashing fashion, where they were formed into a double line by Osterman's assistant and the uniformed officer who had been left on guard by Winston. Slowly they marched past the still form in the embalming room. Some sniffed audibly; others gazed with stolid indiffer-ence, while still others viewed the spectacle with all the cheerful animation that could be expected of a theater audience. Then they filed out through a rear door to as-semble there in little groups and excitedly discuss all pos-sible angles of the affair and the reasons for it. About none of which they had the slightest knowledge.

While Grump eyed the crowd with the chronic suspi-cion of the professional man-hunter Winston called the officer inside.

"Anything happen during the night?"

"No, sir. All quiet."

"The body been identified yet?"

"No, sir. Nobody seems to have seen the girl before. She must be from somewhere else."

"Shouldn't wonder," mused Winston. "By the way, did you have any visitors before six this morning?"

"Yes, sir. Two men. They came in about five and stayed ten minutes or so."

"H'm! Can you give me a description of them?"

"One was a tall, slim feller, dark like a Mexican—"

"Dark, you say?" Winston grasped the officer's arm excitedly and he had hard work to restrain his voice to an ordinary conversational tone. "Think hard, now, and give me the best description of him you can."

"As I said before, he was a tall, slim feller and real dark. He was about thirty, I reckon, and had a little black mustache. I noticed him partic'lar because he was smokin' brown paper cigarettes that smelled like cigars."

"Yes," breathlessly. "And what did the other one look like?"

"I don't remember. He was just an ordinary man in a dark suit."

Winston turned away abruptly and hurried to Grump's side.

"Mike says two men were in to see the body about five o'clock this morning. It isn't likely they had seen a morning paper then. They must have known about the girl's death from other sources. One was a tall, slender man about thirty years old, with a small black mustache and an extremely dark complexion. *And he was smoking brown paper cigarettes that smelled like cigars.* Does that suggest anything to you?"

"Absolutely. That's the sort of butts we found in the ashtray in the Morgan dining room."

"Exactly. And that sort of cigarettes are mighty scarce in this part of the world. I'll bet you couldn't buy a package of them closer than Chicago. The man who came here early this morning to see that body is the same man who smoked and drank in the Morgan dining room last night. I wonder who he could be."

"We'll find out eventually," answered Grump cheerfully. "There never was a puzzle that couldn't be figured out."

Osterman's assistant approached. He was a meek little man with tired eyes and a gray, bloodless face.

"There's something about this case that might interest you, sir," he volunteered rather affrightedly as if he expected to be set upon and severely beaten for his impertinence. "About half past five this morning a man called up and asked if the body had been identified. He has called up about every thirty minutes since."

"You're sure it is the same man?"

"Yes, sir."

"Strange! Wonder why he should be so interested," mused Winston. An idea struck him. "Has he a deep voice?"

"Not especially, sir. Just an ordinary voice but quite cultured and courteous."

"H'm! I'd like very much to hear it. Do you suppose he will call again soon?"

"I should imagine so, sir. It's been nearly forty minutes since his last call."

"I'll wait a few minutes—"

The telephone jangled noisily with a startling suddenness that made the three men jump.

"Perhaps that's him now, sir. I'll see." The assistant picked up the instrument and murmured a quiet "Hello." Then: "Oh! Just a second, please."

He lifted his brow meaningly and Winston leaped to the instrument.

"Hello! You wished to know about the body in Osterman's morgue?"

There was no response. A faint buzzing was all that came to him over the wire. Then he realized that the line was dead. The bird had taken alarm and flown. Winston jiggled the hook frantically until he secured the operator's attention, then demanded a report on the origin of the call. He waited with the 'phone open until it came. The call had come from a booth in a downtown drug store not more than three blocks away.

"He hung up," growled the district attorney disappointedly. "Your asking him to wait must have scared him away. I didn't get to hear his voice. But I will. You stay here, Grump, and look over the crowd. That dark fellow with the strange cigarettes might come back. Or you might pick up some other clue. I'm going to the telephone office. I'll be back within twenty minutes and wait for another call from that chap who is so interested in this body."

"All right, chief. And if any 'phone calls come in while you're gone I'll answer 'em myself."

"Good."

Winston turned to hurry from the building, then stopped abruptly to avoid colliding with a burly figure directly in his path. It was Dodge, the reporter for the *Beacon*. He stood with his feet planted wide, his hands in his pockets, a cigarette drooping from one corner of his hard mouth, his cold eyes boring directly into the district attorney and the latter's two companions just to the rear.

"What are you doing here?" demanded Winston. "Following me?"

"It ain't against the law, is it?" retorted Dodge with an irritating grin.

7

Vanished

The reporter's reply and the impudent way in which he said it angered Winston.

"Just what do you mean by that?" demanded the district attorney.

Dodge seemed to realize that he had gone a little too far. The grin faded from his face and he shrugged.

"Nothing. You wouldn't say anything this morning. But I have to get news and I have to get it however I can."

Winston did not reply. But his eyes smouldered with anger as they remained glued to the reporter. Dodge's explanation sounded all right but he doubted its sincerity. The man's attitude had changed too suddenly. He had the appearance of a man trying to talk himself out of a hole before something was discovered. And his first impudent query had been so filled with assurance. Even now the hint of a sly smile lurked at the corners of his mouth and his narrowed eyes held a humorous glint. Winston felt that the fool was laughing at him. Why? What did Dodge know or think he knew?

The district attorney dropped the discussion abruptly and turned away. He hurried down the street toward the telephone office vaguely uneasy. Dodge's strange attitude not only angered but puzzled him. The devil take the fellow! What could be his object? Then Winston argued with

himself. Why should Dodge inspire the least fear in him?
His own connection with the case was absolutely honorable and legal. Why should he care for its being discovered? But the fact remained that the reporter's smirking
mouth and small evil eyes remained implanted in his consciousness with all the inescapable irritation of a boil on
the back of the neck.

The manager of the local telephone company received
Winston with evident surprise and a trace of agitation.
He was one of that younger generation of business men—
brisk, not to say brusque, painfully efficient, perfect in
the matter of dress and grooming. He rubbed one set of
perfectly manicured nails nervously across his carefully
pressed coat as he waved Winston into a chair, then sat
down on the edge of his own. He smiled weakly and set
out a box of cigars with a hand not entirely steady. A visit
from the district attorney was not to be taken lightly.

"This is an unexpected pleasure, Mr. Winston."

"Unexpected, yes, but I doubt the pleasure part of it,"
retorted Winston with malicious humor. Among the people with whom he came in contact he had the reputation
of possessing the ability to sense unerringly the feelings of
those around him. "But I only want a little information."

"Yes, sir. Anything we have is at your disposal."

"It is about the telephone in the old Morgan home. The
house has been deserted about twelve years. The 'phone
surely hasn't been connected during that time, has it?"

"No, sir. According to our records it was disconnected
in June, 1912."

"Do you remember the details of every 'phone in the
city?"

"No, sir. But I noticed that one in going through the
records a day or two ago."

"When it was ordered connected again, no doubt?" suggested Winston pleasantly.

The young man started and the district, attorney knew he had struck the bull's-eye.

"It is working now," said Winston positively. "When was it connected?"

The manager hesitated.

"You were paid to keep quiet, of course, but twenty-five or fifty dollars wouldn't go very far in hiring a lawyer to defend you on criminal charges," prodded Winston.

"I—I guess that's right," admitted the young man. "It was connected day before yesterday."

"Who ordered it done?"

"A man named Adams. J. S. Adams. I think he was a stranger here. I've lived in Ricksburg all my life but I never saw him before. And he's not listed in the 'phone book or the city directory."

"Describe him." Winston produced a small notebook and pencil.

"He was a large man, tall and heavy. About fifty years old, I imagine. He had blue eyes, a pinkish complexion and a close-cropped brown beard."

"About fifty, eh? Was he gray?"

"His hair was."

"But the beard wasn't?"

"No."

"H'm! I see! Go on!"

"He was very well dressed, inclined to be overbearing and had a deep, commanding voice."

Winston looked up with quickened interest.

"A deep voice, you say?"

"Yes. Quite deep and heavy."

"H'm. What address did he give?"

"The St. Giles."

"H'm! Thanks! If he should return please telephone me. I should like to see him."

Winston could see that the young man was afire with curiosity. But he made no effort to appease it. Instead he slipped his notebook into the inside pocket of his coat and with a calmness he did not feel he walked out of the manager's private office. So the man who ordered the telephone at the Morgan home connected had a deep voice. More than likely he was the same man who had called Thornton the night before from a booth at the Hotel St. Giles.

At the outer door leading to the street Winston stopped suddenly with his hand on the knob. His eyes widened in surprise and he frowned, then his face flushed with anger. At the corner stood Dodge, the *Beacon* reporter, in conversation with a stranger, a lean, alert-looking man with a keen, hard face. And they were staring intently toward the telephone building.

For a long minute Winston stared through the big plate glass window at the two men. It was evident that they were on his trail. Why? Among the numerous questions about the mysterious affair that he constantly asked himself over and over again that was now the most important. Why was Dodge shadowing him? And who was the stranger?

Winston decided to ignore them for the present, to give Dodge enough rope and let him hang himself. In conformity with that decision he hurried from the telephone building without so much as a glance in their direction. He did not pause or glance back until he reached the Hotel St. Giles. Just inside the door he turned back and peered out. Dodge and the mysterious stranger were within a hundred feet of the door. The district attorney's face set grimly and he hurried to the desk.

"Is Mr. J. S. Adams registered here?" he asked the dapper young clerk with the patent leather hair.

The young man looked bored and finally condescended to consult a card file behind a sheltering partition. Then he emerged with an insulted air.

"No, sir."

"Has he been registered here?"

"No, sir. We have no record of him."

"It's possible that he might be registered under some other name," persisted Winston, and he proceeded to outline the description of the deep-voiced man as given him by the manager of the telephone company.

The young man listened with pained attention and at the end of the description emitted a heavy sigh.

"I trust you will realize it is impossible for me to be familiar with the personal appearance of all the St. Giles guests," retorted the young man tartly.

Righteous indignation surged up within Winston. He could feel his face reddening under the pressure. He considered for a moment asserting his authority and demanding more civil treatment, then decided nothing could be gained by such a procedure and hurried toward the door, two dissipated-looking bellboys eyeing him suspiciously.

A flurry at one side caught his attention. Dodge and the stranger, evidently caught unawares by his unexpected approach, were attempting to secrete themselves behind some artificial palms that were part of a number placed at precise intervals about the lobby. For the moment they appeared to be the hunted instead of the hunters. Winston smiled quietly at their obvious confusion, then with sudden decision took the offensive and approached them quickly.

"Hello, Dodge!" he exclaimed in the friendliest manner he could summon. "I'm surprised to find you here. I should think after being up all night you'd need some sleep."

Dodge smiled weakly and attempted to hide his confusion.

"I do—er—I was just going home to get some. But I had to come over here to see—er—a friend. This is him.

Mr. Winston, Mr. Jones. Mr. Winston is the district attorney here and one of our most prominent citizens."

Winston made a quick appraisal of Jones. About thirty-five, slender but lithe, with a lean, bony face, keen, bird-like gray eyes of exceptional hardness that bored through one disconcertingly, a straight, thin-lipped, merciless mouth and resolute chin. A man of decision and determination who would carry through his projects to the end without regard for the means necessary to that end. And Winston felt with vague uneasiness that Jones was appraising him even more thoroughly. He could almost feel the man's uncanny eyes boring into his back as he walked away.

Winston's mind was extraordinarily disturbed as he hurried toward Osterman's undertaking establishment. And there was no apparent reason for it. Dodge had a perfect right to have any friends he wished. And a dozen explanations could be made for his actions. There really was nothing suspicious about the events of the morning when viewed under the spotlight of common sense. Yet Winston could not rid himself of an indefinable feeling of uneasiness. And there was absolutely no intelligent reason for it. He had nothing to be afraid of. But the uncomfortable feeling clung to him as firmly as though a permanent part of his being. For the first time he realized the awful sensations of a hunted man.

Grump was still eyeing the throng at Osterman's when Winston arrived there. The detective was occupying an unobtrusive corner from where he had a clear view of every countenance as it gazed into the still, cold face on the raised portion of the lounge-like affair. Winston quietly made his way there.

"Anything happened?" he asked.

"No. Haven't seen a suspicious action. Have you found anything?"

"Yes. A good many things. I secured some valuable information from the manager of the telephone company. The 'phone at the Morgan home was connected day before yesterday on the orders of a man giving the name of Adams. He had a very deep voice. Must be the same man who called last night for Thornton while we were out there. He gave his address as the St. Giles. I got a description of him and went to hunt him, but they claim he hasn't been there. He—"

The 'phone rang at the back of the room. Winston ploughed back through the crowd in a frantic effort to reach the instrument before anyone else. He did, his eyes shining with anticipation.

"Hello, is this Osterman's undertaking parlor?" came the question.

"Yes," answered Winston, trying to make his voice sound like the assistant's.

"Has the body of the young lady there been identified?"

"Who is this, please?"

"That's of no importance."

"But I must have your name before I can give you any information." Though the voice was strange to Winston, he was making an effort to prolong the conversation so that he might have the tones thoroughly impressed on his memory.

Without another word the other hung up. Winston rejoined Grump.

"It wasn't the man who called Thornton last night. I'm positive I never heard that voice before. But when I asked his name he hung up. Of course he may be only a curiosity-seeker, but I imagine he has a deeper interest than that in this affair. If he has, he'll reappear in the case somewhere and we'll lay a trap so we can meet the gentleman."

"Yeh, I'd like to," assented Grump, his eyes roving here and there through the throng.

"Wonder how the two men we left at the Morgan place are getting along," said Winston suddenly. "They might have seen or found something that would give us a lead. Guess I'll call them up."

He went to the 'phone. Within three minutes he came rushing back and grasped Grump excitedly by the arm.

"They don't answer."

"Don't answer?" repeated the detective bewilderedly.

"No. Something's wrong, Grump. We're going out there immediately."

8

Phantom Footsteps

The two men hurried from the building and climbed into Winston's roadster. As the powerful engine leaped into a throbbing roar the district attorney's right hand reached for the gear lever and his glance swept up the street to gauge nearby traffic. Then he seized his companion's arm.

"Grump!" he exclaimed. "Look there! On the corner!"

The detective's eyes slowly searched the place indicated, then turned back to Winston with surprise in their depths.

"I don't see anything wrong."

"I do. It's Dodge and that stranger. They've been shadowing me all morning. They were in front of the telephone office when I came out. They followed me to the hotel. I almost bumped into them in the lobby as I left. They tried to hide, but I forced the issue and made Dodge introduce his friend to me because I wanted to get a good look at him. Dodge introduced him as Mr. Jones, but offered no further information, though he carefully explained who I was."

Grump's glance had riveted to the two men at the corner while Winston talked.

"He's a stranger here, I'm pretty sure," said the detective at last. "Sort of a hard-looking citizen, isn't he?"

"Rather. I'd hate to be at his mercy. His eyes are like twin daggers. I wonder who he could be."

"May be a city reporter out here to investigate this affair."

"That's possible. Let's drive on and see what they do."

The car shot ahead, the two men being careful to keep their gaze forward until past the corner where stood Dodge and his mysterious friend. Then while Winston drove, Grump leaned out and peered anxiously to the rear.

"They're getting into a taxi!" he exclaimed finally, and there was more than a little excitement in his voice. "They're coming this way. Turn a corner." The car swerved suddenly and he grasped the door to retain his balance. "They turned, too. They're following us, all right."

Winston swore under his breath.

"Whatever their reason for following us, it isn't for our good," he growled through clenched teeth. "I'm going to shake 'em."

"Go to it, boy. I'm with you."

Under Winston's steady, guiding hands the big roadster whirled to the left and shot madly down a side street. Grump stared to the rear and reported the progress of the cab. Its speed was increased accordingly so that it retained its place about one block to the rear. Then Winston allowed the roadster's speed to die abruptly until they were barely moving. The cab, too, slowed. For three blocks they proceeded at a mere snail's pace. Then the roadster stopped entirely.

"What's the idea?" demanded Grump.

"You'll see in a minute. Don't look back."

Winston climbed out and raised the hood. For some moments he appeared to be puttering around with, some of the machine's internal workings, then he lowered the hood and climbed back into his place under the wheel. They went on again, still at the extremely slow pace. Then they turned to the right and drove into a large public garage. Winston leaped out and hurried back to the door. He rejoined Grump with a little smile on his lips and his eyes sparkling with excitement.

"Just as I thought." They think something has gone wrong with my car. They're waiting at the corner for us to come out again. And that's where they miss the boat."

He hurried back through the long lines of automobiles toward the back of the garage. Grump, still mystified, followed, unable to make up his mind as to whether or not the young district attorney's reason had tottered. They came onto a burly man in greasy overalls. A shocking accumulation of dirt and grease could not hide the humorous kindliness of his face. Winston greeted him like an ancient aunt with a million dollars and one foot in the grave.

"Hello, Jack!" he exclaimed joyfully. "I'm going to ask a big favor of you, old top. And incidentally I'll let you in on a little inside information. You probably read in the *Beacon* this morning about that dead woman being found on Twenty-third street. Well, there's a lot more to that case than the general public knows. Grump and I are working on it now. It's one of the biggest murder mysteries that Ricksburg has ever seen. But we want to keep it quiet until we're through and have the guilty people in the calaboose.

"We're going over to Centerville now on an investigation. Some newspapermen have been shadowing us all morning. They're outside in a taxicab now. We want to throw 'em off the track and I felt sure you'd help us. I want to leave my roadster here and drive out the back door of your place in some car that you are willing to lend me for the day."

"Sure, Mr. Winston, I'll be glad to help. I've got a good, powerful touring car here that you can have. I know you'll take good care of it."

Two minutes later Winston and Grump left the garage in a large touring car via the back door. They proceeded slowly down the alley for half a block, then swung into the street and sped rapidly away from the vicinity of the garage. At last they headed for the Lakeview road and the old Morgan home.

"See anything to the rear, Grump?" asked Winston.

"No. It's all clear. We must have shaken 'em. That was a great scheme of yours, but why did you tell that fellow we were bound for Centerville?"

"Because Dodge will question him eventually when they get tired waiting and at last enter the garage. Jack wouldn't willingly give me away, yet Dodge has a reputation for browbeating people into telling things they never intended to tell. But no man can give information he doesn't possess."

"That's so, too. And now let's step on it and get out to that old rookery. I'm anxious to find out what's happened to those two harness bulls."

"So am I. But that's not the only thing I'm anxious about. This fellow Dodge is beginning to get on my nerves. I can't understand why he's following up this case so relentlessly."

"I don't see that his actions up to now are out of the ordinary. I think he just smells a story behind the finding of this body and he intends to follow it up and beat the *Clarion* on it."

"Maybe you're right, Grump. There may be nothing at all behind his strange acts, but I can't get rid of the idea there *is.*"

The old Morgan home was less repulsive in daylight than at night but equally ugly. The big house was badly in need of paint, and here and there a shutter hung awry on one hinge; or some other obvious sign of neglect revealed itself shamelessly. The once beautiful grounds, now an impenetrable wilderness, emphasized the desertion and decay which the old place represented so eloquently. And over all hung a silence that it seemed sacrilegious to break. It was like invading a tomb.

In spite of the bright sunshine Winston and Grump both felt a little awed by the weird setting for this inexplicable mystery. As they ascended to the porch it seemed that they pounded their heels needlessly hard as if to bolster up their own courage with noise that would cut through the ominous silence enveloping the place.

Winston opened the front door and entered without knocking, the detective at his heels. In the tense silence their own breathing sounded terrifyingly loud. But nothing else came to their anxious ears. They forced themselves into the rooms on either side of the hall. But no sign of the officers could be found.

"Wonder where Murphy and Harrison are!" exclaimed Winston irritably.

"Asleep somewhere most likely," answered Grump contemptuously.

"Not after that scare you gave them before we left last night." He raised his voice: *"Ho Murphy!"*

His shout rang through the house, echoing and re-echoing down the long, empty halls, into the deserted rooms, and rushed back at him increased ten-fold. Then it diminished until it died away and the awful silence of complete desertion settled down over the gloomy old house again. There was no answering call. Winston shivered slightly, and even the cold-blooded, nerveless Grump glanced about apprehensively.

"Bet I was right," growled the detective.

"I hope so," answered the district attorney fervently. "Let's search the house."

Both were armed with revolvers and powerful flashlights and they began a systematic search of the house. The ground floor came first. One after another they went through the rooms. Dust. Shrouded furniture. Close, musty air. And silence. In the kitchen they got a shock. The stove contained a quantity of hot ashes. The sink was filled with dirty dishes and three uncleaned skillets.

"Somebody had breakfast here!" exclaimed Winston.

"Bet it was Murphy and Harrison. They'd rather eat than sleep and rather sleep than do anything else."

"Maybe. But where'd they get the stuff?"

A close search of the kitchen followed Winston's question. They found the big cupboard amply stocked with a large quantity of groceries and canned goods.

"Somebody was ready for a siege," remarked Grump.

The first shelf in the cupboard was about three feet from the floor. Below it was ample room for a medium-sized man to sit in comfort. One corner contained a heap of matches, cigarette stubs and ashes.

"Looks like some man was in hiding here," mused Winston.

"Yes. But why in the name of heaven would a man in hiding smoke? Cigarette smoke carries a long way."

"I know. But here's the evidence. And it was neither of the men we found traces of last night. These cigarettes are just a cheap domestic brand."

Grump turned his attention to the sink.

"Looks like there were five people," he concluded. "There are five plates, knives and forks. . . . Were there any dishes in the sink when you came here last night?"

"I don't remember. I paid but little attention to the kitchen because I considered it of no importance."

"You never know what will prove to be important," answered Grump in gentle reproof.

They went into the dining room. Everything was as it had been the night before at the time of their first investigation. The table was not disturbed. None of the dishes or silverware used by the unknown persons had been taken from there. All thirteen places were complete.

"Funny they didn't use these dishes," mused Grump. "It would have been so much handier than to hunt for others."

"That's just another of the thousand 'funny things' about this affair," mused Winston grimly.

They went on to the front of the house. They had reserved the fatal library until last, and they entered it now not without hesitation. In his mind's eye Winston could see that inert figure stretched out on the floor at his feet. Grump stared uneasily at the window where the face had appeared. Then they both gasped aloud. Some fifty books, the entire contents of two shelves, lay on the floor in a careless heap. Some were closed and lay flat. Others stood on end, half-open. Still others were spread wide like a bug that has been stepped on. The heap looked as if the volumes had been removed and examined one at a time then dropped to the floor to lay wherever and however they landed.

"Looks like a cyclone had hit 'em," observed Grump.

"Do you suppose this is the work of Murphy and Harrison?"

Grump laughed shortly.

"Not a chance! Murphy can barely sign his name. He couldn't read a third-grade reader much less any of these books. And Harrison ain't much better. No, you can be sure they never bothered any *books!*"

Winston started to speak but the words died to a hoarse gasp in his throat while his jaw hung a-gape and his eyes widened apprehensively. Grump, too, was staring fearfully at nowhere in particular, his face ludicrous with amazement and terror. Winston seized his arm suddenly and he jumped a foot off the floor.

"Do you hear that?" asked the district attorney.

"Y-y-yes," answered the detective.

They stood silent and motionless, listening intently. Aged footsteps, faint but unmistakable, were ascending stairs somewhere, slowly and with frequent halts. And at intervals came a low, slithering rumble, as though the possessor of the eerie feet were dragging a heavy body along behind him.

9
X

Grump mopped the cold perspiration from his brow with a trembling hand as the phantom footsteps died away to nothingness. He cleared his throat twice before he could force his vocal cords to function.

"Lord! what was that?" he gasped. "Spooks or human?"

"Sounded too real to be spooks," observed Winston slowly. "But there was nobody around—at least not that we could see."

"I've always been able to see anybody that was close enough for me to hear 'em walk," answered the detective drily with a nervous glance around the room. "And I want to keep on doing it."

"But sight is a matter of light." There was a humorous twinkle in Winston's eye as he began to expound a scientific theory he had heard at some time or other. "There are bodies so lacking in various elements that they are not solid enough to reflect sufficient light for us to see them. Some of the spiritualists say that is the reason we can't see the earthbound souls or spirits that are around us all the time."

"*Brrr!*" Detective Grump shivered and looked quickly behind him as though he expected to find a demon there ready to leap upon him. "That's too deep for me. Let's do something."

"All right." Winston was secretly amused at the imperturbable Grump's evidence of fear when faced with occurrences beyond his comprehension. "We'll search the house."

They did—in a thorough though somewhat hesitant manner. The huge dark rooms with their abnormally high ceilings, their musty air and their massive, old-fashioned furniture gave one the impression of weird tombs, redolent with history and long undisturbed. There was something forbidding about them that made the intruder hesitate. They were rooms that seemed made to harbor murder.

Winston drew a quick breath as he entered one of the bedrooms slightly in advance of Grump. The detective crowded forward and immediately saw what had caused the district attorney's surprise. The covers of the big bed were thrown carelessly back, the sheet and pillow rumpled.

"Somebody slept here recently," snapped Grump with the rapid-fire deduction for which he wished to be noted.

"So it seems," answered Winston drily. He paced slowly about the room. "Ah! Look here!"

Grump joined him. On the dresser was a dish-like piece of bric-a-brac of ancient appearance, containing a quantity of ashes and easily a score of stubs of the long, slender, brown paper cigarettes filled with cigar tobacco.

"Evidently this is or was the room of our foreign friend with the mania for distinctive cigarettes," observed Winston.

"He might have come up here only to see someone else."

"Yes. He *might* have. But I don't think so. It would be necessary for him to be here some time to leave so many cigarette stubs, and they're all fresh, as you can see."

After that, Grump led the way into all the rooms. He had not the slightest fear of anything human, and now that the case seemed to be taking a turn toward practical things he intended to be in the forefront when the solution was reached.

They found another bedroom which had been occupied recently. And on the dresser they discovered a tiny bottle of an expensive perfume imported from Paris. Which led them to suppose that the occupant there had been a woman and a fastidious one, too. But there was no other clue.

They went downstairs more puzzled than upon ascending to the second floor. They had found no trace of the two missing policemen. Neither had they discovered anything which threw light on the matter of the phantom footsteps.

"What in the devil could have happened to those two men?" demanded Winston irritably as they re-entered the library. "It does seem that two strong, able-bodied, armed policemen would be able to take care of themselves."

"They probably went to sleep," said Grump cynically. "And whoever made away with 'em merely had to tie 'em up and throw 'em down a coal chute or a well or somep'n'."

He strolled moodily around the room, his eyes roving about the floor. Pausing suddenly, he dropped to his knees and stared intently at the rug for some moments. Then he whipped out a magnifying glass and stretched out flat on the floor, supporting himself by his elbows while he examined the rug through the glass. Winston watched with uncomprehending interest.

"Here's a clue," said the detective finally without looking up. "A lot of ashes and several grains of Murphy's tobacco."

Winston hurried forward and joined him on the floor, gazing through the glass at the important spot.

"You're right," admitted the district attorney at last. "But are you sure it's Murphy's tobacco?"

"Positive. Not a man in a thousand smokes that strong, coarse, black stuff. It's terrible. I tried some once at headquarters when I ran out of my own and it sent me home to bed staggering. That's Murphy's, all right. Evidently the gold dust twins spent some time in this room before they were made away with."

"So it seems," mused Winston.

His glance was roving about the floor, as though the carpeted surface could explain the mystery which faced them. Suddenly it riveted to some dark stains which stood out prominently against the plain gray surface of the expensive rug. Without a word he seized the glass unceremoniously and examined the spots. Then he beckoned excitedly to Grump.

"Look here! What do those spots look like to you?"

Grump stared long and earnestly through the magnifying glass. Then he looked up, his eyes shining with the light of discovery.

"Blood!" he snapped grimly.

"Exactly. The question is *whose* blood?"

Grump rubbed a forefinger firmly across all the stains but it came away clean.

"All dry," he said ruminatively. "Been there some time. Might be the girl's—the one you found dead here last night."

"Not a chance. She'd been strangled. There were no wounds."

"Then it's somebody else's," retorted Grump brightly. "It's up to us to find out whose."

"You don't suppose Murphy and Harrison were murdered?" hazarded Winston with a breathless little catch in his voice.

"I don't suppose anything without evidence," answered the detective a trifle snappishly. "Let's see if we can find any more clues."

He turned his attention to the pile of books. Winston followed his lead. Volume by volume they went through the heap, not certain as to what they hunted, but searching on in dogged attempt to find something of importance. The examination proved that the heap of books was not the result of carelessness or an accident. The volumes had not only been thrown to the floor but torn apart with ruthless vandalism. Covers and backs were ripped open with an apparently aimless desire to destroy. But Winston's face was grim with thought. At last he turned to Grump.

"It looks to me like whoever is responsible for this mess was hunting something—something which he or she thought was inside some of these books."

"I hadn't thought of that," admitted the detective grudgingly. "It sounds reasonable though. But what could you hide in the cover or back of a book?"

"Papers."

"That's so. It's about all that could be hidden there, too. I wonder if the thief found what he was hunting."

"I'm afraid so," said Winston. "Otherwise there would be more books here."

The two men continued their self-imposed task with renewed interest, searching carefully for the possible empty hiding place. They reached the bottom of the heap without any additional discovery. But there, on the floor, they found a revolver, a regulation police gun of .38 calibre. And it contained six empty cartridges.

"Not so good," mused Grump as he fondled the weapon. "There's nothing on this gun to identify it, but I'll bet it belonged to Murphy or Harrison."

"Whoever it was evidently used it," answered Winston. "Must have been a battle here before they were put out of the way."

"Looks that way. But what could cause it?"

"Some of the mysterious people connected with this strange affair probably wanted to get in here at these books and the police had decided to use this room as headquarters. The only thing to do was fight it out. Our men evidently lost."

"So it seems," agreed Grump grimly. "They may have paid dearly for their defeat, too. But where could they have been disposed of?"

"There are endless answers to that," retorted Winston. "They may be on the grounds of this estate. Or they may be right in this house, spirited out of sight through a secret panel."

"All good possibilities. The last two we can investigate ourselves."

A close examination of the room followed. No traces of a secret panel were found in the walls. But bullet holes were, seven of them, some five feet from the floor and all clustered near the doorway. Two more could be seen in the ceiling, while half a dozen missiles had penetrated the wall which had been exposed by the disarrangement of the books.

"Some battle!" exclaimed Grump grimly. "The boys defended themselves, anyway."

"But it evidently didn't do them much good. Must have been more than one of the enemy."

"There's nothing more we can do here. Let's look around outside."

A thorough search of the entire estate produced no discovery save further extensive proof of the total decay into which the once magnificent place had fallen. Windows of the outbuildings were broken out with jagged irregularity; the doors hung slack or rusted, broken hinges, offering but little opposition to stray winds that entered stealthily and stirred up strange rustlings and eerie echoes in the darkest corners. The grounds were a ragged unkempt wilderness, altogether hideous and almost impenetrable in spots, with a great deal of the pity-inspiring quality which the sight of neglected age stirs in any human heart.

Returning to the house after the fruitless search, Winston's keen eyes brooded on the tower-like projection which stood out at the left front corner of the building. It was made of brick like the balance of the house, the mortar beginning to crumple from age, but completely smooth and solid with no sign of an opening, terminating some ten feet above the shingled roof of the house in a peaked cupola. Viewed under ordinary conditions it would have been accepted as an integral part of the building, one of the useless ornamentations which were inflicted on homes years ago. But Winston regarded it with suspicion. He remembered distinctly that none of the rooms contained a round side to conform with the exterior contour of the tower. And it was large, at least ten or twelve feet in diameter. It could contain many things. Stairways. Secret rooms. Caches of valuables. Barred prisons for animals or men. Torture chambers. Wracked skeletons. The bodies of the two missing policemen. Winston's active mind conceived any number of awful possibilities.

"I don't like that tower," he said finally.

"Neither do I," assented Grump. "Looks like hell. What would a man want with a thing like that on his house?"

In spite of the seriousness of his thoughts, Winston smiled.

"That's what I've been trying to figure out the last few minutes, Grump. Let's see if we can find an entrance to it."

They couldn't, though they spent an hour in the search. None of the rooms nor even the cellar offered a means of entering the mysterious tower, which surely had some purpose and might contain anything.

"There must be some secret panels in this house," said Winston with conviction as he paused to mop his perspiring and dust-smudged face. "No man would spend money on a thing like that without a reason. It's big enough to contains small rooms or almost anything else. The possibilities it offers are endless. Yet there is no visible entrance.

That's beyond all reason. Evidently old man Morgan wanted to keep its contents a secret. But I'll bet a hundred to
one that he had some means of getting into it himself."

"Seems like he would have. Must be a secret panel
somewhere."

They hunted until both were so irritable that neither
would trust himself to speak to the other. It was a simple matter to see which walls adjoined the tower. But all
appeared to be solid. Not even a hollow sound could be
wrung from them by constant hammering. They returned
to town, puzzled and angry.

Winston's secretary rose to meet him as he entered his
office in the city hall.

"A boy brought this note about a half hour ago," she
explained.

Winston tore open the envelope impatiently and hast-
ily scanned the single sheet of paper. Then he looked at
Grump.

"Listen to this!" he exclaimed excitedly. "Dear Mr.
Winston: You have in your possession a carnation which
I wish to obtain. This plain flower cannot possibly be of
any value to you but it is of great value to me for personal
reasons. Therefore please drop this flower in the mail box
at 1432 West 23rd Street. Do this personally and be sure
you are not watched by the police if you value your life. I
have this day deposited to your credit in the First National
Bank the sum of five hundred dollars. An equal sum will
be placed to your credit as soon as practicable following
your compliance with my request. If you do not comply I
shall take other steps to secure the flower. X."

10

A Warning

"Well what do you think of that?" demanded the young district attorney as he stared at the note following his reading of it to Grump.

"I think it is one of the best clues we've found," answered the detective quickly. "The address given there should be something good to work on." He joined Winston and stared at the note. "Woman's handwriting."

"Yes. A refined woman, too. And well educated. Accustomed to the best, judging from the paper."

"And from her offer. It isn't every woman who can pay a thousand dollars for a carnation, regardless of how bad she might want it."

"I wonder if there is anything to that offer or if it is merely a joke?"

"Phone the bank."

It was a good suggestion and Winston followed it. He turned away from the telephone after a short conversation with the cashier obviously more puzzled than ever.

"It's true!" he exclaimed excitedly. "The money is there to my credit. It was deposited about two o'clock in cash—five hundred-dollar bills—by a woman, a large, well-dressed brunette of middle age who did not give her name. The bank people noticed her carefully because of her unusual act. But she was a stranger to all of them and hurried out of the bank at once without giving any explanation of her conduct. The cashier says she seemed much agitated."

"She's a new one in this mix-up. We haven't run across her before."

"Well, she's evidently in earnest about this offer of hers for that carnation I found in the library of the old Morgan home not far from the body of that dead girl. But why should she be so anxious to regain possession of it?"

"To get a clue leading to her out of your hands. Undoubtedly this woman was in the Morgan home the night of the murder. In some way she lost this flower and you got possession of it before she discovered her loss."

"That's logical, all right. But why, should she be so anxious about an ordinary flower?"

"Perhaps it isn't an ordinary flower. There may be something distinctive about it that you didn't notice."

"That's possible," admitted Winston and went to his desk. He unlocked the top drawer and produced the flower. Grump seized it, his eyes drinking in avidly its every detail. Disappointment grew in his face. The carnation seemed to be just an ordinary blossom.

"No clue here," said Grump at last. "I don't see why that woman should be so anxious to get it back. There's nothing to distinguish it from a thousand other carnations."

Winston was gazing narrowly at the crushed, wilted flower.

"What about the color?" he asked finally. "I don't remember of ever seeing one that exact shade before."

Grump stared ferociously, at the blossom, turning it over and over in his fingers. He had no more knowledge of flowers than the average man. That is, he knew a red one when he saw it or a white one or a blue one. There were not more than a half dozen varieties that he recognized at a glance. But now that his attention was called to the fact he could see that this carnation was different from every other carnation he had ever seen. Its basic color was a distinctive ivory white but the crinkled petals were plentifully splotched with a vivid red that stood out like bloodstains. Before he thought, Grump rubbed his forefinger across the blossom then looked up a trifle shamefacedly.

"It does seem to be a different shade," he admitted. "I never saw white look just like that—at least, in a flower."

"Maybe that's the secret," retorted Winston. "Take it down to Knull's and see if you can get any information about it."

Grump pocketed the flower and departed hurriedly for the town's leading florist. Winston paced nervously around his office for a few minutes then informed his secretary that he would return within half an hour and went back to Osterman's undertaking establishment. The afternoon paper, on the street an hour before, had played up the case in great style and the lines of people were filing past the still form in undiminished numbers. Winston sought out the assistant in the tiny, meticulous office over which hovered a vague, medical smell.

"Has the body been identified yet?" asked the district attorney.

"No sir. And we've had a tremendous crowd here all day. As you probably noticed, sir, there are two policemen on duty. And there have been times when we needed another." The undertaker's assistant was a small old man with brooding, washed-out eyes under high, arched brows and the slightly sagging facial muscles of a man chronically in need of sleep. He seemed to take a gloomy delight in the widespread interest which the case had created. "Nobody seems to know the girl. She must have been a stranger here."

"Looks that way," admitted Winston. "Yet I'm not so sure about that. Somebody here must have known her.

There's usually a pretty definite reason for a murder. Perhaps the people who knew her consider it to their interests to keep her identity a secret."

"That's possible, sir. So many strange things happen nowadays."

"Has that mysterious man who refuses to give his name kept up his telephone calls?"

"Yes, sir. At almost regular intervals of half an hour."

"Has he said anything new?"

"No, sir. Just the same thing. 'Has the body been identified yet?' And when I say 'no' he hangs up." He paused as the telephone at his elbow rang. "Osterman's Mortuary." Then a pause. "No." He hung up and turned back to Winston. "That was him again, sir."

The district attorney seized the instrument and ordered the operator to trace the call. In a moment, evidently galvanized into unusually rapid action by his brusque tone of command, she reported the desired information. The call had come from a pay booth in a drug store only three blocks away. Acting on a sudden impulse Winston rushed to the drug store. He found only employees of the establishment present. But he knew the proprietor, who happened to be in.

"Have you noticed a man doing a lot of telephoning from your booths today?" asked the district attorney.

"Yes. He's been in at least a dozen times. He never stays but a moment, though."

"Ever seen him before?"

"No. I think he's a stranger here."

"What does he look like?"

"Tall, slim, blonde chap. Well-dressed. Looks English or perhaps Scandinavian."

"Speak good English?"

"Perfect."

"What sort of an impression does he give?"

"Good. Seems to be extremely intelligent. Very polite, almost too much so for an American."

"You have no idea what his business is?"

"No. But I can tell you this much: he makes a living with his head instead of his hands. That's evident. He might be anything from a duke or a bond salesman to a professional crook."

"Thanks. There's a reason which I'm not at liberty to disclose just now why I want to talk to this chap. And the only way I can do it is through you. Will you help me?"

"Absolutely."

"Good. I thought you would. What I want to do is to put one of the city detectives into your store until this fellow comes in again. Oh, he'll come, all right. No need to worry about that."

"Where'll I put your detective?"

"Behind the counter as a clerk. He won't do you any good, of course. And I hope he won't do any harm. I'll pick an ordinary-sized man. You can fit him up with a white coat, can't you?"

"Sure."

"Fine, I'll send him around at once. I don't think he'll have to be here more than an hour."

Winston hurried to headquarters, personally selected a detective from those on duty and dispatched him to the drug store with emphatic orders to bring the mysterious blonde stranger to the city hall as quickly as possible. Then the district attorney returned to his office in the most cheerful frame of mind he had experienced since the morning of the ill-fated Marie's first note.

Grump was already there, pacing the floor like a caged animal and twisting his defenseless hat into inconceivable shapes. He leaped for Winston like a dog after a bone and almost dragged him into the private office.

"Looks like you've found something," said Winston.

"Found something!" snapped the detective. "Rather! No wonder that dame wants her carnation back. Knull says it's a very rare kind—just developed last year by some English hor—horti—oh damn it! flower-grower. It's called the 'Queen Mary.' Knull saw some at an exhibit in Chicago last spring. He hasn't got any himself. He says they're very expensive and that only the finest florists in the big cities would have them."

"Which would indicate that this mysterious woman who calls herself 'X' is wealthy and a stranger in Ricksburg."

"And mixed up pretty deep in this murder. Don't forget that!"

"I won't. We're not through with her yet, by a long shot. Now Grump, send telegrams to the florists' associations in Chicago, St. Louis and Kansas City, asking them for the names of their members who have carnations of this sort and request them to give us, if possible, the names and addresses of people these carnations have been sold to within the past month. Get the technical name of the flower from Knull before you wire. Tell them that it is official and urgent and sign my name and title to the messages."

Grump hurried away with the irresistible eagerness of a blood-hound who has caught the scent. Winston reflected in silence for a quarter of an hour then consulted the city directory and the telephone book. He could find but three Thornton's, a plumber, a policeman, and a banker. He had his secretary telephone all three, requesting them to call at his office as soon as possible on an important matter. Then he turned his attention to various business which had accumulated during his absence from the office.

Ten minutes later he answered the telephone in response to a signal from his secretary in the outer office.

"Hello," said a vaguely familiar voice. "Mr. Gerard Winston? This is a friend speaking. Never mind who. Just a friend— For your own good, drop immediately the investigation on which you are now engaged. This is final."

Winston hung up when he realized the line was dead. That warning was ominous. It gave him a little tingling sensation at the roots of his hair. He had recognized the voice before the connection was broken. It was that of the deep-voiced man who had called the Morgan home the night of the murder and asked for Thornton.

11
Mixed Trails

Winston impatiently awaited Grumpy return. He wanted the detective's opinion and advice before making any move in response to the threatening telephone call. Grump was not a great detective when it came to deduction and theoretical crime detection but he was a capable officer who shot straight and hard and without asking too many questions. Winston was beginning to feel that he would need a man of that sort by his side until the present investigation was finished.

The moment Grump returned to the office, Winston acquainted him with the telephone call. The detective listened in amazed silence. Then a heavy frown gathered about his eyes.

"Do you think there is any significance in that threatening call coming so soon after you had summoned all the Thorntons to your office for questioning?"

"Can't say. I'll know about that after I have questioned them."

"Of course. You can see how they act . . . Did you trace that call?"

"Yes. It came from a booth at the St. Giles. All of his calls have come from there. He surely must be a guest at the hotel. Wouldn't it be a good idea to put one of the boys over there to watch for him?"

"Sure. It won't do any harm anyhow. And it might help things a lot if we could pick him up." The detective turned to go.

"Just a minute, Grump," called Winston. "I wish you would conduct a little personal search of your own for this man, also for that dark fellow who smokes the funny cigarettes and for the chap who has been calling Osterman's all day. I got a good description of him from Brann, the druggist. He's been calling from there."

And Grump departed in search of the two men whose description he had under his hat. He was to place another detective at the telephone booths in the St. Giles to keep a watch for J. S. Adams, with the deep voice, then go on a personal hunt for the two men who had indicated plainly their connection with the mystery.

Winston remained in his office, awaiting the Thorntons. But though his body was inactive, his mind wasn't. It raced about here and there in no definite fashion like a dog at play with a ball. A hundred ideas, possibilities, explanations, threw sand in the wheels of his mental processes. He wondered about that threatening call. Had it been meant in earnest? These men had proven their earnestness with one murder. They undoubtedly would not hesitate at another to gain their ends, whatever those ends might be. For the thousandth time he wondered what was behind the whole affair, what was at the bottom of this murder and all the other mysterious circumstances that had followed?

With sudden vexation he realized that the detective on duty at Brann's drug store had not reported, although considerably more than an hour had elapsed since he had assigned the man to that post. The telephone brought him into immediate communication with the officer. The detective's report was discouraging. The blonde man who had telephoned Osterman's Mortuary at regular intervals of half an hour all day long had not been in the drug store since the detective had assumed his post there.

Winston telephoned Osterman's. The assistant informed him that the mysterious inquirer was still making his calls at the customary intervals. The last one had come in less than ten minutes before. It was evident that the inquisitive stranger was calling from some other place. Did he know of the trap Winston had laid for him? It appeared that way.

The district attorney turned away angrily from the instrument, lighted a cigar and strode to the window. Then he tensed and drew back. In the street below were Dodge, reporter for the *Beacon,* and the strange man he had introduced to Winston as Jones, and they were engaged in earnest conversation with another stranger, a hard-looking middle-sized man of evident sporty inclinations. After talking a few moments they hurried away, all departing together.

"Damn!" exclaimed Winston. "I wish I knew what Dodge was up to."

He turned away from the window as the door opened to admit his secretary.

"A Mr. Thornton to see you, sir," she explained.

"Fine. Send him in."

Winston sat down behind his heavy desk and assumed a somewhat ferocious attitude for the cross-examination which was to follow. He realized that the first impression was most important. If he could disconcert his visitors from the start and keep them on the defensive he would probably learn much more than if he allowed them time and attention to formulate explanations and alibis.

The first of the three Thorntons to answer the summons to the district attorney's office for questioning was the policeman, a fat, flabby man of middle age with sleepy blue eyes and a kindly red face. He was still in uniform and appeared extremely ill at ease as he accepted Winston's gruff invitation to be seated and gingerly sat down on the edge of a chair.

"Where were you last night, Thornton, from ten o'clock until two this morning?"

"Why—why at home, sir."

"Sure of that, are you?"

"Yes, sir."

"You could prove it if necessary?"

"Absolutely, sir. By all my family and Jack Callahan, who boards with us."

"Well, you were expected to be somewhere else, weren't you?"

"No, sir, not that I know of. I went off duty at five-thirty last night and walked directly home. I didn't leave there until seven this morning."

"You weren't expected to be at the old Morgan home on the Lakeview road about one o'clock this morning?" persisted Winston sharply, leaning forward in his chair and boring the officer with a cold, direct glance that obviously disconcerted the man.

"No, sir. I never was near that place in my life. And I don't want to be. If you'll pardon me sayin' so, I don't get you at all, Mr. Winston. Would you mind telling me what this is all about?"

"Sorry but I can't, Thornton," answered the district attorney. "All I can tell you is that it is about that girl who was found dead on Twenty-third street last night. Have you been down to Osterman's to see her?"

"Yes, sir."

"Ever see her before?"

"Not that I remember, sir."

"Incidentally, do you know of anybody named Thornton who was connected with the Morgans when they lived here years ago?"

"No, sir, I don't."

"All right, Thornton, that will be all. Thanks for coming up."

The policeman departed, evidently mystified almost to the point of doubting Winston's sanity. The district attorney took a turn around the office and lighted another cigar. There was nothing to be learned from Patrolman Thornton. It was evident that he knew nothing of the Morgan case or much of anything else.

Grump arrived within a few moments, much discouraged, judging by the expression on his perspiring face. His first words confirmed Winston's worst fears.

"Nothing doing, chief," admitted the detective. "I've tried to get a line on those two birds in every way I know. But it's like tryin' to dam Niagara with mud. They're strangers, all right. But that's all I can find out about 'em. They must be livin' in a cave out in the woods."

"Looks like we're up against a clever bunch, doesn't it?"

"Rather! I'll bet this isn't the first crime they've been in on. They're clever, and I don't mean maybe."

"All the more glory to landing them when we finally do," retorted Winston calmly.

"*If* we do, you mean."

"No. *When* we do."

"You're my idea of an optimist."

"Don't get discouraged, Grump. We'll get 'em. It's just a question of time. We're finding more clues every hour . . . . There are three Thorntons in Ricksburg. I've summoned them all here for questioning. One, a policeman, was here just a few minutes ago. He didn't know a thing. But I expect the other two here before long. Stick around and see what they have to say. We might find something good."

The door opened. It was the secretary again. Another Mr. Thornton in the office.

"Send him in," directed Winston and took refuge behind his heavy desk.

The second Thornton to answer the district attorney's summons was the plumber, a brawny man in greasy work clothes with a bullet-shaped head whose ugliness was accentuated by being shaved entirely nude. He came in truculently with his heavy jaw thrust forward and his small eyes squinted.

"My wife says you want to see me," he growled, ignoring Winston's invitation to be seated.

"Yes," answered the district attorney crisply. "Just want to ask you a few questions."

Quickly he put the man through about the same cross-examination as he had the first Thornton. But it was immediately apparent that the man knew nothing of value on anything, much less the mysterious affair at hand. Winston allowed him to depart within a very few minutes.

"Nothing doing there," admitted the district attorney as the plumber closed the door behind him. "There's one chance left—the banker. Somehow, I'm rather hopeful about him."

Banker Thornton arrived within ten minutes evidently agitated. He was puffing as though after a fast walk and he applied a gay silk handkerchief to his forehead at frequent intervals. He sank into a chair with obvious relief and fanned himself with his hat.

"You wanted to see me, Mr. Winston?" he asked nervously.

"Yes."

The district attorney studied him frankly, silently, deliberately. The old banker shifted under the steady stare and his eyes flickered. As one of the financial czars of Ricksburg, this sort of treatment was new and unwelcome to him. He was a small, dapper man, in the late sixties, meticulous, almost dandified, in dress. His head was completely bald save for a fringe of white hair and had a pinkish tinge. His face gave one an immediate impression of shrewdness. The eyes were small and of a piercing blue, set far back in their sockets under beetling white brows and surrounded by networks of wrinkles from much squinting under the stress of thought. The nose was long and thin and sharp; the mouth below it grim and ruthless, with thin, bloodless lips and shaded by a carefully clipped white mustache.

"There are some questions I want to ask you, Mr. Thornton," began Winston slowly. He realized that in order to secure any information of value from this man, he must handle him differently from the other two. "You knew Mr. Morgan when he lived here years ago, didn't you?"

"Yes. Slightly."

"He was wealthy, wasn't he?"

"Yes."

"Did you know anything of his personal affairs?"

"No. No. No. He was very close-mouthed about such matters." The banker's nervousness under the questioning was evident.

"Morgan had a daughter, I believe?" said Winston suddenly, changing his line of questioning.

"Yes."

"How old would she be now?"

"About twenty-one, I think."

"Do you remember her name?"

"I—I believe it was Marie."

"H'm!" Winston's tone was significant. His eyes were gleaming with heightened interest. Out of the tail of his eye he could see Grump shifting about uneasily in the corner.

"Now, Mr. Thornton, I have a very personal question to ask you. I trust that you will realize that I ask it in the interests of justice and consequently will not resent it. *Where were you from ten o'clock last night until two o'clock this morning?*"

The banker jumped as though suddenly connected with an electric wire and made three attempts to speak before he was successful.

"At home—in bed—of course." He tried to be indignant.

"You could prove that if necessary?"

Thornton's face swelled with anger.

"Your impertinence is insulting, young man. Of course I could prove it."

"I don't doubt your word, Mr. Thornton," answered Winston soothingly. "But weren't you *supposed* to be out at the old Morgan home about midnight?"

"No. Absolutely not. I won't—er—that house has been closed for years." He rose and clamped his hat down on his head furiously. "I won't submit to any such high-handed questioning any longer," he shouted and stormed out of the office.

"Want me to bring him back?" asked Grump tensely,

"No." Winston was smiling coldly. "I'll talk to him again later when he's cooled down a bit."

"Do you think he knows anything?"

"I'm not sure yet." He paused as the door opened to admit his secretary with a yellow envelope. Winston tore open the message with a pounding heart. There is something dramatic about any telegram and this one might mean the solution of the whole puzzle. His gaze swept over the sheet then he looked up at Grump, his eyes shining with excitement: "Listen, Grump: 'One of our members, H. H. Kraly of two-twelve east Madison street, sold one dozen of special carnations you inquire about to Doctor H. R. Sherwood of sixty-four-thirty-seven Lawndale avenue on the twelfth. Chicago Florists Association.' By God, Grump, that's the man we caught prowling about the grounds of the Morgan place last night after the murder!"

12

Enter Mr. Jensen

Grump leaped to his feet with grim decision.

"I'd better go out now and get him before he takes a notion to fly the coop."

"Not so fast, Grump!" counseled Winston crisply. "Let's talk this thing over first. If the Sherwood named in this telegram is the same man we found prowling about the Morgan grounds last night, it begins to look as though? he were involved in this case. But before we take any action we must wait to hear from St. Louis and Kansas & City."

Replies from both cities arrived within fifteen minutes. Both florists' associations were emphatic in denying that any of their members had ever possessed any of the rare carnations.

"That leaves it up to Sherwood!" exclaimed Grump. The mere thought of an impending capture imbued him with the sense of glee which any officer feels when about to close in on his quarry. "I'm telling you, chief, we'd better land him before he finds out we're after him and makes a getaway."

"Suppose we should arrest him," assumed Winston. "What could we do with him? Ask him questions and try to make him incriminate himself further? But if he refused to answer—and from what I saw of him last night I'm positive he would—I'd be compelled to release him. We have nothing on him. But he would have something on us then. He would have an idea of what we were doing and the information would be communicated at once to the others involved, provided he is in on it. To arrest him now might wreck the whole case and destroy all our chances of solving this mystery."

"Well, what are you goin' to do, then?" demanded Grump petulantly. He felt that the ultimate reward of a detective was to clap the hand-cuffs on somebody and when he was denied the privilege he felt as if he had been cheated of his just desserts.

"I'm going to comply with the request of this mysterious 'X'," answered Winston calmly. "It is evident that she—I'm positive it is 'she'—is involved deeply in this affair. I aim to set a trap which will deliver her into our hands. I shall take this carnation which she considers so valuable and leave it in the mailbox at the address she gave. Then I shall drive away as though I were obeying her instructions to the letter. But you and another detective will be watching. And you'll watch until somebody tries to get that carnation. Whoever it is will be taken into custody here immediately for a severe questioning. And he or she will be held. I have enough evidence in the note alone."

"But that means a lot of risk for you," objected Grump. "You know what the note said: 'If you value your life '"

"I know. But that can't be helped. 'Nothing ventured, nothing gained.' I must assume the risk in order to get results."

Grump shrugged. "All right. It's up to you." His face set suddenly in hard, grim lines. "But if anything happens to you there's goin' to be a lot of crooks take a quick trip to hell."

Thus it was that half an hour later a small car with side curtains on proceeded slowly up Twenty-third street and finally came to a stop across the street and down two houses from number 1432. A man alone behind the wheel clambered out, procured a small black grip from the tonneau, ascended the steps of a certain house and was admitted after ringing the bell. The most astute observer would never have suspected that Detective Grump and one of his most able colleagues were crouched low in the tonneau, guns in hand, expecting the worst and ready for it.

Fifteen minutes later Winston's fleet roadster dashed up the street and ground to a halt noisily squarely in front of number 1432. The young district attorney climbed out, glanced about nervously then hurried up to the porch. A moment he fumbled about at the mailbox then hurried to his car and drove quickly away. But even in that short space of time he had learned that the house was vacant. Elation welled up within him as he drove back to the office. 'X' would surely be compelled to come out into the open to gain possession of the carnation. And he knew he could rely on Grump to obey orders.

Back at the office, Winston tried to turn his attention to other work. But his mind, busy in spite of himself with the problem at hand, refused to concentrate on anything else. He took to pacing around and around his office, smoking furiously, his face set in a perplexed frown, one hand nervously rumpling his hair.

Fifteen minutes passed. Thirty. Forty. And finally an hour had crept by. Winston swore under his breath. What could be the matter? It seemed as if his best plans, the traps on which he was relying to clear up the mystery, were coming to naught. He whirled suddenly, his eyes shining with sudden anticipation, as the door opened. It was Grump—alone. And the detective's face indicated failure.

"Sorry, chief," he began slowly, narrowly watching his superior. "But we got gypped. After you left, Tom and I waited and waited. But nothing happened. I had a hunch

that something had gone wrong so I had Curtis go over to
the house with his little grip as though he was canvassin'
for something. He looked in the mailbox and the carnation was gone."

"Gone?"

"Yes. Slick as a whistle. And I'll swear that nobody
went near that mailbox after you left it until Curtis did.
Tom'll back me up. And so will Curtis. He was watching
from the house where he stayed."

"You're sure the flower was gone?"

"Curtis said it was. He looked carefully. He said there
was no back in the mailbox and that the wooden wall of
the house seemed to have been sawed through. Looks like
this crowd is willing to go to any lengths to accomplish
their purposes."

"Yes," answered Winston slowly. "There must be something big at stake."

"Wonder what it could be?"

"We don't know—yet. And there's no use guessing.
Well, Grump, go back out to that house and wait around
awhile. See what you can find. Go on down and take a
look at six-fourteen, too. Same street. That's the address
Doctor Sherwood gave us last night. See what's going on
around there. But don't make yourself too evident? He'd
probably recognize you."

Grump hurried out and Winston sank into the chair
behind his desk, tired and puzzled. When this case was finally known to the public as it must be eventually it would
be the making of him politically if he should unravel it
and bring the guilty people to justice. It would assure him
another term as district attorney or it might mean a judge-
ship. From there it was but a short step to state senator
and then governor. After that—but he refused to go any
further for it seemed as if he were a long way from solving
the initial problem at hand.

He looked up expectantly at a heavy knock and called an impatient "Come in."

The door opened and two men entered. Winston's heart leaped as he recognized them. One was Detective Price; the other a tall, slender blonde man of foreign appearance.

"Here's the chap who has been calling from Brann's drug store all day," explained the officer. "All the men there identified him."

"I should like to know the meaning of this outrage," snapped the stranger in very precise English.

Winston surveyed him with frank curiosity. It was evident that the man in custody was furious. His youngish, handsome face was tense with anger; his blue eyes snapped with cold fury; his small blonde mustache fairly bristled above his angrily grim mouth. His large, well-shaped hands twitched nervously as though anxious to grasp something and rend it apart.

"*I* will ask the questions," retorted Winston sharply. "Why have you been calling Osterman's Mortuary all day to find out if this dead girl's body had been identified?"

"That's my business."

"Very well. That girl was murdered. Perhaps you'd be interested to know that you are deeply involved in the case and that it would be greatly to your advantage to tell me anything in your favor."

"And if I choose to remain silent?"

"You will spend considerable time in jail and more than likely end up on the gallows." Winston realized that here was a difficult man to handle. Ruthless methods were necessary. And a great shock right at the beginning might have a salutary effect.

It did. The stranger blinked under the district attorney's last thrust. Two deeply-cut parallel lines between his brows indicated profound thought.

"Will you take my word for certain things?" he asked finally.

"Perhaps."

"Will you consider any statements I make with an unbiased mind?"

"Yes."

"Then I'll tell you what I know of this affair. It isn't a great deal but it may be of interest to you."

"And it may save you a lot of trouble."

"I am a dealer in antiques—"

"And your name?"

"Thor Jensen. The firm is Jensen and Jensen of New York. My brother and I."

"Have you a card?"

"Yes." He produced one, an expensive, engraved affair bearing an imposing address in the fashionable east fifties.

"Go on," prompted Winston quietly and dropped the card into his desk drawer.

"About two weeks ago a young woman came into our shop and asked to talk with a member of the firm. I was present and responded. She was handsomely dressed and evidently a person of wealth and refinement. She gave the name of Marie Morgan."

"Marie Morgan!" gasped Winston, hardly able to believe his ears.

"Yes. She said she had been willed an old house out in the middle west which she intended disposing of together with its contents as she was to marry soon and go abroad to live. She said this house contained a large number of antiques and described some of the pieces. I could see that she must have some real treasures and agreed to meet her here in Ricksburg yesterday. I arrived at nine-fifty in the morning and registered at the St. Giles as she had requested me to do. But I heard nothing from her all day. And this morning I read in the paper about a body being found. The description sounded as if it might be she. I visited the morgue and felt sure the body was that of the woman who was the cause of my being here. Yet I couldn't be positive and I've waited all day hoping that I was mistaken and that Miss Morgan would get in touch with me."

"H'm! And why haven't you come forward with this story before?"

"Because I did not wish to become involved, even slightly, in the affair. I even went outside the hotel to telephone my inquiries to the mortuary."

Winston turned to Detective Price, who had remained near the door, an interested listener.

"Did you 'frisk' this man?"

"Yes, sir."

"Find any weapons?"

"No, sir."

"Anything else of interest?"

"No, sir. But there's one point I would like to mention. He says his name is Thor Jensen. But the initials inside his coat are H.L.T."

Winston tensed suddenly like an animal about to spring. And his gaze bored into 'Jensen.'

"Is that true?" he demanded.

"You bet it's true," retorted the detective before the stranger could answer. "Here! Look for yourself!"

He stepped forward and jerked open the man's coat. There, sewed by the tailor to the lining just below the opening of the inside pocket, were the initials; H.L.T. Winston stared like a man hypnotized. The last initial fascinated him especially. 'T.' This man might be 'Thornton.'

"I'm sorry, Mr. Jensen," he said slowly and there was biting sarcasm in his tone. "But I shall have to keep you in custody until this affair is solved. Take him to jail, Price."

13

Attempted Murder

Seven o'clock found Gerard Winston, dinner forgotten, still in his office pondering over the Morgan affair. He had been on the point of believing Jensens' story and releasing him when Detective Price had volunteered his surprising information—information which seemed to definitely disprove the stranger's statements and involve him deeper in the case because of his having lied.

That story had sounded so devilishly plausible. It had held firm under the ruthless spotlight of the most devastating analysis of which he was capable. He was still wondering about that story, wondering if it could possibly be true. It was reasonable. It fit in surprisingly well with his own ideas and theories about the case. It confirmed his opinion that the murdered girl was Marie Morgan. It corroborated his theory that the girl had returned to Ricksburg for some unknown reason and had been murdered because of her mission.

He looked up with sudden suspicion as a quick knock sounded at the door. His hand crept toward the black, ugly automatic that was always in the desk drawer immediately in front of him. The cold steel against his fingers sent a quick shock through his nervous system. His eyes brightened with anticipation.

"Come in!" he snapped.

His mouth set grimly as he recognized the figure that entered. It was Dodge, the reporter for the morning *Beacon*. And his ugly face was still screwed up into that gloating smile that somehow made one want to wipe it off with a clenched fist.

"Well, chief, how are you this evening?" he began cheerily. "Got anything more to say about this murder case?"

"No," growled Winston.

His tone was sufficient to acquaint any man with his state of mind but Dodge, unabashed, pushed his derby hat far back on his head, dropped into a convenient chair and lighted the stump of a cigar cocked up in one corner of his crooked mouth.

"How about this fellow Jensen?" he prodded.

Winston tensed angrily. His eyes snapped warningly.

"So you know about that, eh?"

"Absolutely. I'd be a damn poor reporter if I didn't. I had a very interesting interview with him. It'll make a good story too. And now I'd like to have your side of the case."

"I have nothing to say."

"Then I'll have to print only his side. And it's a hot one."

"Print what you damn please!" snapped Winston. This case was already getting on his nerves and Dodge was deliberately goading him for some unknown reason. "Sign your article. Then people will know it isn't so."

He expected Dodge to go raging out of the office at that. Nothing of the sort. The reporter remained irritatingly cool. Only his eyes narrowed shrewdly.

"All right, old top, if that's the way you feel about it. But if you were willing to talk I might be able to exchange some valuable information with you."

"What sort of information?"

"Oh, various things," answered Dodge evasively.

"Be specific."

"Not unless you will."

Winston had cooled as abruptly as he had grown angry. He wondered if it was Dodge's game to anger him. A man mad oftentimes said things which he wouldn't dream of saying in a different mood.

"There's very little to tell about this man Jensen," he said suddenly. "Only that I feel he is involved in the affair rather deeply. He told me a certain story which I don't believe so I am holding him until I can investigate."

"Have you any evidence against him?"

"I don't feel at liberty to say. That's all I can tell you."

Dodge rose. "Thanks. Good night." He started for the door.

"Hold on!" exclaimed Winston. "What's the information you had for me?"

"Sorry, but I don't feel at liberty to tell," answered the reporter with malicious humor and a knowing wink. "That's all I can tell you."

He hurried out, leaving Winston in anything but a pleasant frame of mind. The district attorney was worried and his face showed it. Somehow Dodge made him uneasy for no apparent reason. But what had he meant by 'exchanging valuable information'? Had he found out something startling that he was keeping to himself? It was a problem that Winston found himself unable to solve. But he had an uneasy feeling that he and Dodge were far from through with each other over the Morgan mystery.

Grump came in a few minutes later, obviously tired and discouraged.

"Couldn't find a damned thing," he admitted disgustedly. "The house where you left the carnation has been vacant about three months. I talked to the agent who has charge of it. Says the people who own it want too much rent. I examined the place carefully. The back door was open. Lock broken. Curtis was right. Whoever got that carnation sawed through the front wall to get at the mailbox. Must have done it before you got there and you didn't notice the cuts."

"Did you find out anything about the Sherwoods?" asked Winston anxiously.

"Yes. Made some cautious inquiries from the neighbors. Sherwood is a superintendent at the mill. Has a good job. Moved here from Chicago five years ago. They live well but not extravagantly. Wife's well liked. They seem to be perfectly respectable people in every way. This Doctor Sherwood is his brother. Lives in Chicago but has been there visiting three or four days."

"No clues then, eh?"

"Not a one. Looks like we struck a blank wall there."

In the fewest possible words Winston outlined his interviews with 'Jensen' and Dodge.

"This 'Jensen' sounds to me like hot stuff!" exclaimed Grump. "We'll give him a good going over in the morning."

"Rather," assented Winston grimly.

"Haven't heard anything from Murphy and Harrison?"

"No." A sudden impulse struck Winston. "Let's go out to that old rookery tonight and hunt them."

"I'm game if you are."

"All right. Let's go."

They had an ample meal at a nearby restaurant then sped toward the old Morgan home. The Lakeview road was a main highway and at that hour of the evening carried heavy traffic both east and west. Winston was compelled to hold down his speed as he threaded in and out among the long lines of cars.

A car of evident power roared up from behind and came parallel with the district attorney's machine. He and Grump had a quick view of two men in the front seat, dark, frowsy men with sullen faces shaded by low-pulled caps. Then the car started around with a sudden roar. Under the driver's skillful manipulation it cut in ahead of Winston's machine then slowed abruptly, half turning crosswise of the road.

Winston was acting even before Grump's warning shout rang in his ears. Automatically he jammed on the brakes and swung the wheel. But his speed was greater than he realized. And the ditch was closer. The brakes screeched indignantly. The car lurched and skidded to the right. The wheels on that side reached beyond the edge of the highway and the heavy machine toppled over into the ditch. The car that was the cause of the accident roared away.

Winston crawled out from under the steering wheel and surveyed Grump, seated in the soft mud of the ditch.

"Hurt?" he demanded with a wry smile.

"No. Are you?"

"The steering wheel jammed my chest a bit. But it's nothing serious."

"That's good." Grump clambered to his feet, his clothes plentifully plastered with mud. "Looked to me like those fellows deliberately tried to wreck us."

"It's possible. They were hard-looking customers. Did you get their license number?"

"Yes. You stay here with your car. I'll commandeer a machine and see if I can't run them down."

Already the highway was choked in both directions from cars stopped to see what had happened. People were crowding around, staring horrified at the overturned car, then awe-stricken at Grump and Winston as if they were returned from the dead. Grump leaped into a machine with an obviously unwilling man and they rushed away, blowing the horn furiously to clear a path.

Winston swore under his breath and rubbed his bruised chest. A puffy man with inquisitive pop eyes ambled up with the calm self-assurance of the trained business luncheon speaker.

"Have a wreck?" he inquired complacently.

"No. Just decided to park there in the ditch," retorted Winston impatiently and turned away.

Another motorist, recognizing Winston, volunteered assistance. The district attorney requested him to telephone a garage to send out a truck and the man hurried away. The crowd, realizing that no further sensation was forthcoming, began to disperse.

To Winston, pacing the edge of the highway, it seemed hours before Grump returned. And then the detective's search had been fruitless.

"Couldn't find any trace of 'em," he admitted disappointedly. "And we went at least five miles beyond the Morgan place. But they had a pretty good start and there are at least a dozen crossroads they could have taken. But I've got the number of the car. We may be able to track them down with the help of the state highway police."

"I wonder if that was an attempt to get me," mused Winston.

"I think so," answered Grump grimly. "Those fellows looked to me like Chicago gangsters. I'll bet they're part of the crowd we're after for this murder."

The truck from the garage arrived in charge of a boy unbelievably greasy and apparently glorying in his uncleanliness.

"Had a wreck, eh?" he said happily and surveyed the overturned car with a professional eye.

"I believe she'll run all right once we get her back on the road," he said finally. "Don't look to be busted much."

The derrick on the back of his truck pulled the heavy roadster out of the ditch as easily as a powerful man could have retrieved a child's wagon from the same position. Winston climbed in behind the wheel and depressed the starter pedal. The engine coughed then roared into life. He threw in the clutch and pulled the gear lever. As he slowly released the clutch pedal the car moved forward as smoothly as ever. Save for the bent fenders and liberal decorations of mud it was the same as before.

"There's no use in going on out to the Morgan place," said Grump. "I passed there. And it's as dark as pitch. Can't be anybody there."

They raced back to Ricksburg and in the office of the chief of police looked up the license number of the car which had caused the wreck. The machine was the property of a local garage. A telephone call there confirmed the fact. The car had been rented early in the evening by two strangers who had not given names or addresses. But they had put up without a murmur a two-hundred-dollar cash deposit on the car. The machine had been returned in good condition some twenty minutes before.

"Ain't that hell!" exclaimed Grump disgustedly.

"It is," agreed Winston. "But there's nothing we can do about it now. We've made some progress today anyhow. Let's get some sleep and attack the case with fresh minds in the morning."

Winston dropped off to sleep almost the moment he climbed into bed. But it seemed as if not more than half an hour had elapsed before Hallud awakened him. The negro's eyes were wide; his face mirroring tremendous agitation.

"Wake up, massa," he commanded excitedly. "De warden ob de jail jus' phoned. He say tell you quick dat a man name' Jensen has escaped."

14

More Clues

Winston seized a dressing-gown and rushed for the telephone. Within two minutes he had the warden of the jail at the other end of the wire. That gentleman was highly excited. It was the first time in the history of Ricksburg that a prisoner had escaped after once being locked up. It was a terrible occurrence but had been carried out with great cleverness, evidently by professional crooks who were experienced in jail-breaking. He hoped that Mr. Winston would not think it was his fault.

"Cut the preliminaries!" snapped the district attorney. "And give me the details. What happened? And when?"

"Carrington, the night jailer, discovered the escape, sir," answered the warden shakily. He seemed afraid that Jensen's escape would mean his immediate dismissal. "He passed the cell about six o'clock just as it was getting light. The bunk seemed to be empty. He stopped and peered in, using his flashlight to see better. The bunk was empty. So was the cell. Then he saw that bars over the window had been sawed through. He telephoned me and I called you as soon as I had completed my investigation."

"Do you think the prisoner could have made his escape alone?"

"No, sir. He was thoroughly searched before being placed in the cell. Somebody must have helped him during the night."

"Very well. You and Carrington be at my office at ten o'clock. We'll have to have an investigation about this escape." Winston hung up, then called police headquarters. "Lieutenant Carter? District Attorney Winston speaking. Late yesterday evening I committed to jail a man who gave his name as Jensen—Thor Jensen. Yes. In connection with this mysterious dead girl. He claimed to be a member of the firm of Jensen & Jensen, antique dealers of New York City but the initials in his coat were H.L.T. I've been looking for a man named Thornton in connection with that case and I thought he might be the man. I was holding him for further investigation. But he escaped during the night. Yes. The bars over the window of his cell were sawed through. The warden thinks he must have had outside assistance. Send out a general alarm for the whole force to be on the lookout for him. Here's his description. Give it to the county highway police, too. He may try to escape by automobile." Winston gave the Lieutenant in command at headquarters a description of Jensen supplying every detail he could remember. "Grump around there yet? No? All right. Do everything you can to get Jensen. I want him. But do it quietly."

Winston then called Detective Grump's home.

"Hello, Grump? This is Winston. Jensen escaped during the night. Yes. Hainline called me up a few minutes ago. He thinks there must have been outside assistance. The bars over the cell window were sawed through. I've summoned him and Carrington to my office at ten o'clock for an investigation. In the meantime, I wish you would go down to the jail and see what you can find. Then report to me before ten. I've already called Carter at headquarters and told him to send out a general alarm for Jensen."

Winston shaved and dressed in record time, reaching the table before Hallud was ready to serve the breakfast. But the *Beacon* was there, ready for his attention, and he

picked it up with a frown as he remembered Dodge's overbearing tactics in trying to secure news. A streamer headline in large black type caught his eye, *Winston Holds Suspect.* A lengthy article followed in Dodge's unmistakable
style, in which many insinuations were made. It hinted
broadly that there was something big behind the murder
of this mysterious girl and that Winston knew a great deal
more than he was telling. Jensen's story was given in full,
including his direct statement that he knew nothing whatever about the case and his accusation that he was being
persecuted. The article hinted that there must be a reason
for Winston handling an apparently innocent man thus and
as much as said that the reason wouldn't look well in print

Winston dropped the paper with an angry snort as Hallud entered with a tray. He was almost finished with his
meal when the doorbell rang. Hallud hurried out, then
came Robinson's voice in the hall.

"Come on into the dining-room, Mr. Robinson," he
called.

The reporter for the morning *Clarion* came in softly, as
meek and downcast as ever.

"I hope you'll pardon me for coming here and at this
time," he began uncertainly. "But I wanted to see you before you got to the office. I wondered if there wasn't something about this case that you might prefer to tell me
privately and I could use as much or as little of it as you
wished. I would protect you absolutely."

"I know you would, Robinson. But there really isn't
much that I can say at the present time."

"Dodge has a good story in the *Beacon* this morning."
He seemed rather resentful about that.

"Yes. But he didn't get any of it from me."

"Who is this man Jensen?"

"Frankly, I don't know. The *Beacon's* story tells you who
he *says* he is. But I doubt that. He telephoned Osterman's

Mortuary all day yesterday at regular intervals of half an hour to inquire if the girl's body had been identified. I traced his calls, found out where he was phoning from and had him taken into custody. He was very indignant. Claimed he had no connection with the case. I couldn't get a thing out of him. He said his name was Thor Jensen but the initials in his coat were H.L.T. Which indicated to me that his name was something else. But here's a point that you can scoop Dodge on because your paper comes out before his next edition does: Jensen escaped during the night from the city jail."

"He did?" Robinson leaned forward, excitement visible in the flickering of his pale blue eyes behind the thick-lensed glasses. He reached for a crumpled wad of copy paper and a thick, stubby pencil. "How'd he do it?"

"I don't know yet—exactly. But the bars across the cell window were sawed away. Hainline, the warden, is positive that he had outside assistance. That's all I know now but I have summoned Hainline and Carrington, the night jailer who discovered the escape, to my office at ten o'clock this morning for an investigation on the matter. If you'll drop around about eleven I may have something more for you."

"Thanks ever so much, Mr. Winston. I shall do that."

He rushed away to begin work at once on the most exciting story he had been able to write for a month.

Winston finished his breakfast hurriedly and drove to his office. He was relieved to find that his car seemed to be none the worse after the wreck of the night before. He felt that its escape was accidental, as was his own. He was fully convinced that the occurrence had been attempted murder.

Grump was awaiting him at the office.

"Find anything interesting?" asked Winston.

"Nothing special. The bars were sawed through, all right. Three of 'em. It would have taken quite a while and made a lot of noise. Carrington must have been asleep. I think Hainline is right about the outside assistance, though. They did a neat job, too. It would have been easy for anybody to get to Jensen. He was in a ground floor cell."

"No clues at all, eh?"

"Only one." Detective Grump reached into his coat pocket, then extended his hand toward the district attorney. Winston's eyes focused on the small object in the other's fingers, then grew wider as he recognized it. It was one of those rare red and white splotched carnations. And it had the same crumpled, lifeless appearance as had the other one.

Winston looked up, still turning the small blossom about in his fingers.

"Significant, don't you think?"

"No doubt," assented the detective. "I wonder if that's the same flower that escaped us yesterday afternoon."

"Perhaps. It looks to be. But we can't be certain. At any rate it is one of the same kind. And as rare as they are, it is sure to be a link in this case."

"But where could it have come from? It wasn't in Jensen's possession when he entered the cell."

"It might have been on one of his helpers, becoming dislodged during the rescue and left on the cell floor unheeded or unseen in the hurried flight. Or it may have been left behind deliberately as a gesture of defiance. Some master criminals always leave a 'card' of a distinctive nature wherever they visit on 'business'."

"That's so. I hadn't thought of that."

The telephone bell rang and Winston leaped for the instrument. He set it down a moment later with a sharp click and turned back to Grump.

"Lieutenant Carter says an attempt was made during the night to burglarize old Henry Thornton's house. Patrolman Simpson just made the report. Hurry over to headquarters. Get all the details. Find out why Simpson didn't report the occurrence earlier. Interview Thornton and find out all you can."

Detective Grump hurried away. Winston hung up his hat with a strange slowness, then sat down quietly in the comfortable chair behind his big desk. His elbows found a resting place on the polished surface of the desk and he placed his fingertips together with a preoccupied precision. His clear, gray eyes held a dull, faraway look indicating profound thought. Banker Thornton's house burglarized. The citizenry of Ricksburg included no one with the requisite nerve to attempt such a thing. They would be afraid of recognition in case of discovery. Therefore the job must be the work of an outside criminal or gang of them. And outside criminals made forays of such a nature only for a very definite purpose—for large potential profits, and after extensive investigation and preparation. Ricksburg contained half a dozen houses which offered much greater possibilities in the way of valuables than that of the conservative, unostentatious banker, Thornton.

The investigation produced no additional evidence in regard to Jensen's escape. Carrington, the night jailer, could add nothing to his first statement and Hainline, the warden, knew nothing except that he was extremely fearful of being dismissed because of the occurrence. Winston sent them away after a sharp reprimand and an ominous injunction to be more careful in the future.

Robinson returned promptly at eleven, eager for additional sensation which was not forthcoming. Winston dismissed him rather more shortly than he deserved and attempted to turn his attention to other work. Without success. His mind kept reverting to the attempted robbery of the Thornton home. Was there something special that the thieves wanted? And why had the officer waited a matter of hours before reporting it? Above all, where was

Grump? He should have completed his investigation and been back long before.

It was only twenty minutes before noon when Detective Grump arrived, flushed and breathing heavily as though he had been running. Winston sat up straight and his frown disappeared. It was evident that the sleuth had discovered something of importance.

"Oh, what a morning!" he puffed finally. "I hope we don't have another case like this soon."

"Come on, man! Tell me what you've found!" snapped the district attorney impatiently. "It seems as if I've been waiting for you a month."

"And it seems to me as if I've been chasing around a month. Simpson had left headquarters when I reached there and I had to go out to his house. He said about three o'clock this morning he was standing on the next corner from the Thornton place. Everything was dark and extremely quiet There was a sudden crashing of breaking glass. The sound seemed to come from behind him and he hurried back along the street, keeping his eyes and ears open. Suddenly he saw a man dash out of the Thornton grounds. He gave chase and shouted a command to halt. But the fellow kept going and escaped in an automobile."

"Did Simpson shoot at him?"

"Yes. Three times. Thinks he winged the intruder, too. He says the fellow was limping when he reached the car."

"Was there anybody else in the car?"

"He couldn't tell positively but he thinks there must have been because it shot away the instant this other bird reached it. He went back to the house and found that one of the library windows had been smashed out. The room was torn up quite a bit as though the intruder had been searching for something. Old man Thornton was looking around the room. He had a revolver and was very much excited. Said he was awakened by a noise and, coming downstairs, found a burglar in the house but the fellow escaped before he had a chance to shoot. Simpson asked to use the phone to report to headquarters and Thornton talked him out of it. Said nothing had been stolen and that he didn't want any publicity. Ended up by giving Simpson a twenty-dollar bill and telling him to forget it. But Simpson got to thinking about it this morning and decided he ought to report anyhow."

"Did you see Thornton?"

"Yes. But he was awful grouchy. Wouldn't say a word. Said he didn't want to hear any more about the matter."

"H'm! Well, he may talk yet and be glad to. Did you get any description of the burglar?"

"No. Couldn't. Simpson said he couldn't see him clearly because of the darkness and Thornton said the fellow got away before he saw him."

The door opened and Winston's secretary entered with a folded newspaper.

"A boy just came with this," she volunteered. "He said it was for you."

A puzzled frown settled over Winston's face as he took the paper and examined it. It was a copy of the morning *Beacon*, folded so as to expose the want-ad page. A heavy blue line encircled an item in the 'Lost and Found' column:

> LOST. Small, thin, all-metal pocketknife of distinctive design. Made by Hinkle Bros, of Germany. Has little intrinsic worth but owner values it highly as a keepsake. Liberal reward will be paid if returned to Austin J. Barksdale, 506 Citizens Bank Bldg.

15

Identified

Winston handed the paper to Grump.

"Read that!" he commanded.

Puzzled, the detective's eyes absorbed the little item. But when he looked up his eyes were sparkling with interest.

"That must be the knife you found in the Morgan home the night of the murder. And somebody wants it back. Who's this Barksdale?"

"An attorney here. Sly old fox. He has a good enough name but I don't think he would ask too many questions about a dollar that was coming his way."

"Do you suppose he is involved in this affair?"

"Can't say. I wouldn't be surprised one way or the other. The only thing to do is investigate."

Grump rose. "Want me to do it?"

"No. I'll go myself. An officer would make him suspicious. He may have good cause to suspect 'em. But I know the old boy and I can probably do as much with him as anybody. Wait here for me unless you get a call from headquarters about this case."

Austin J. Barksdale was a difficult man to analyze. He was decently cordial in welcoming Winston to his office but the district attorney had an uneasy feeling—more of a subconscious premonition—that the man wanted to jump at his throat. But one couldn't be sure either one way or the other. He had the sort of face, oftentimes found on lawyers and bankers, that is a living lie. It showed neither excessive warmth nor excessive coolness. In fact it registered no definite emotion at any given time. His smile, one felt, was merely a mechanical gesture, springing not from any spontaneous desire to smile but a deliberate command to his muscles given only after extensive thought on the matter. Every movement, every expression, seemed to have a purpose—a sinister purpose. He gave the impression of being in possession of great and incriminating knowledge. He seemed always on the verge of attack.

In stature he was tall and slender, not with the supple, alive slenderness of athletic youth but with the hollow, bony slenderness of decadent age. His face was distinctive but somewhat repellant. The forehead was wide and high, topped by a thinning thatch of carelessly tended gray hair; the features prominent and sharply cut. The eyes were small, keenly blue, heavy-lidded and shrewd, not humorously shrewd as are those that serve as windows for a kindly, optimistic soul, but coldly shrewd, reflecting the frosty fires of a harsh, starved, merciless soul if a soul can claim such qualities. Further they were placed far back under wrinkled, heavy lids that seemed to serve as dense veils, protected by bushy brows of mingled black and gray; set rather too close together on either side of a long, high-bridged, hawk-like nose that terminated in an inquisitive point just above a wide, tight, thin-lipped mouth which descended in a straight fall to an angular, pointed, ruthless jaw.

"This is an unexpected pleasure, Mr. Winston," he said with an artificial cordiality evidently summoned for the moment. "Sometime since we've met. My loss, I assure you. Won't you sit down?" He rubbed his thin, bony, paper-white hands together as Winston accepted the proffered chair, the long slender fingers intertwining with sinister facility unpleasantly reminiscent of strangling something. "Have a cigar. . . . How are things going?"

"Very well," answered Winston noncommittally. He lighted the offered cigar with his eyes riveted to the other attorney. Barksdale gave the impression of nervousness, without any definite motion or expression indicative of such a state. "I noticed your ad in the paper this morning," said Winston suddenly. "That's what I came up about."

Barksdale stiffened abruptly and the heavy lids automatically lowered over his hard eyes.

"Yes?" His fingers were toying with a slender, keen-bladed paper knife.

"Yes," answered Winston shortly. "The ad was called to my attention in a rather mysterious manner—in a way that would indicate *someone* felt positive I had that knife in my possession."

"Why should anyone think that?"

"I'm sure I don't know. But the truth of the matter is, I did find a knife recently which is of rather distinctive appearance."

Barksdale's eyes flickered with quickened interest. He leaned forward, extending an eager hand.

"Let me see it." His tone was suave but held more of a command than a request.

"Later," parried Winston quickly. "Give me a description of it first."

"You saw the description in the paper this morning, didn't you? It was quite explicit, I'm sure."

"Yes. But I should like to hear it from you. The description in the paper was only general and it is the little details that count."

The attorney's lips pressed together with grim firmness. His gaze was riveted immovably to the paper knife which was now clenched in his fist. Then he relented suddenly, and turned back to Winston.

"It was a small knife, extremely thin, and made entirely of metal. The handle is covered with a scroll design, and the trademark of the manufacturers, the famous Hinkles of Germany, is embossed on either side."

"What does this trademark look like?"

"A pair of tiny, grotesque twins hand-in-hand."

"Is the knife rusty at all?"

Barksdale stiffened and the heavy, wrinkled lids drew lower over his hard eyes.

"I really couldn't say," he answered shortly.

Winston pounced with the speed and sureness of a mongoose seizing a cobra.

"Then it isn't your knife?"

"No," snapped Barksdale, furious at having been trapped so neatly.

"Whose is it?"

"That is a private matter and must remain so," answered the attorney stiffly.

"Not if you hope to recover that knife," retorted Winston grimly.

Barksdale leaped at the opening.

"Then you have it?"

"Yes. But I refuse to relinquish it—yet."

"Then I shall take other means of recovering it."

"Do, please, and you'll find yourself involved in the biggest murder case Ricksburg has had in years."

Barksdale's eyes flashed.

"Just what are you insinuating?"

"I'm insinuating nothing. I'm merely stating that I consider this knife an important clue in the death of this mysterious girl. You've read about it in the papers, no doubt." There was enormous irony in Winston's voice. "I have the knife in my possession and I intend to keep it until the man who owns it can prove to my satisfaction his innocence of any complicity in the affair."

"I shall take the matter up with my client and advise you. I had no idea that any such condition existed."

"I should much prefer to interview him personally."

"That would be quite impossible."

"Not necessarily," answered Winston coolly. "The law has many things at its disposal."

"Is that a threat?"

"No, a plain statement of fact."

"But I am positive that he will be glad to come forward and answer any questions you may wish to ask."

"I hope so—for his own good. Incidentally, Mr. Barksdale, there are a few questions I wish to ask you."

"I shall be glad to answer any that I may—properly." The attorney's manner was anything but eager.

"You have lived here quite awhile, haven't you?"

"Thirty-eight years."

"You knew the Morgans, then?"

"I had a speaking acquaintance, with Colonel Morgan, yes." Barksdale was answering slowly, apparently choosing his words carefully.

"Who handled his legal business here?"

"I did, what little there was of it. I think most of his affairs were administered somewhere in the west."

"You don't know where?"

"No."

"Wealthy, wasn't he?"

"Quite so."

"How'd he make it?"

"I haven't the slightest idea. He gave one the impression, though, of being a man of the open. Mines, perhaps. Or ranching."

"Did you draw his will?"

"I did not."

"Were you acquainted with its provisions?"

Barksdale sat up a little straighter. His right hand was clenched so tightly around the handle of the sharp paper knife that his knuckles seemed about to punch through the white, cracked skin. He had the surprised, set, half-stupid look of a man who has just received a stroke of paralysis.

"I was not," he said at last. His voice was low and tense. "Colonel Morgan was a very close-mouthed man."

"I've heard so. Who was his banker?"

"Thornton of the First National."

"H'm!" The corners of Winston's mouth quivered slightly as though he were restraining a smile. "Colonel Morgan died quite suddenly, didn't he?"

"Yes. Almost mysteriously, one might say. He fell dead just before dinner one evening. Hadn't been sick a day and seemed to be feeling fine up to ten minutes before his death."

Winston leaned forward with renewed interest.

"Was it any special occasion?"

"Yes. His birthday. A large number of his relatives were present for the occasion. Cocktails were drunk and within five minutes the old gentleman dropped dead."

"Was there no suspicion of foul play?"

"No. But the superstitious people in Ricksburg talked about it for a long time because the table had been laid for thirteen."

"For—thirteen?" gasped Winston.

"Yes. And the funny part of it was that only twelve people were present."

"Including the family?"

"Yes, including everybody. It was the general supposition that someone else was expected who didn't come."

"Were any relatives missing from the group?"

"Several, I believe."

"Who were they?"

"I can't say."

"You mean you don't know or you can't tell?"

"I don't know," retorted Barksdale sharply.

"Very well. Thanks for the information you've given me. And please get in touch with your client at once about that knife. It's quite important to all of us."

Grump was still waiting in the district attorney's private office when Gerard Winston returned after his interview with Austin J. Barksdale.

"How'd you come out?" demanded the detective anxiously as Winston threw his hat on the desk and sank into his chair.

"Yes and no," answered the young district attorney. With a deliberation that was maddening to the other he bit off the end of a cigar and struck a match. "Barksdale is a pretty close proposition. It's something like cross-examining an alligator. I found out a few things though. In the first place, it isn't his knife. It belongs to a client of his whom he won't name. Said he would get in touch with the man and that he felt sure he would come forward and submit to questioning. Which I doubt very much. But I've still got the knife. In the meantime I want Barksdale shadowed every minute. We may run onto something valuable in that way. If any of these people we suspect show up around his office or he goes to see any of them I want the whole bunch brought here at once."

Grump jumped to his feet.

"All right, chief. I'll see if I can't nail the old codger with the goods. I'll bet he knows more about this case than he lets on."

"Shouldn't wonder. By the way, Grump, I found out something else. He used to be the Morgan attorney here and Thornton was their banker. How does that sound?

"Good. We'll unravel this thing yet."

"Absolutely. It's just a question of time."

Grump hurried away. Almost immediately the telephone rang. It was the bank. Another five hundred dollars in cash had been deposited to Winston's credit a few minutes before by the same heavy-set, middle-aged woman who had made the first deposit as a guarantee of good faith in the matter of the rare carnation which he had found on the floor of the Morgan library the night of the murder.

Winston mentally kicked himself as he hung up and turned away from the instrument. Why hadn't he set a watch on the bank, set a trap for the mysterious 'X' who was willing to pay a thousand dollars for the return of a single carnation? In the rush of other things he had forgotten it and regrets would avail nothing now.

Within five minutes the telephone rang again. Winston answered impatiently but expectantly. His face tensed as he recognized the voice of Osterman's assistant.

"The body has just been identified, sir, as that of Marie Morgan," came the thin, squeaky voice. "Her brother made the identification."

"Very well. Thanks. Get the policeman on duty there and have him bring young Morgan to my office at once. It's very important."

16

A Body Blow

Though in virtual custody, young Morgan seemed willing enough to submit to questioning from District Attorney Winston. He shook hands cordially and talked freely with apparent frankness. He was a tall, clean-cut chap in the late twenties, well dressed and evidently accustomed to the best of everything.

"You are a son of the late Colonel Morgan who was for years a resident of Ricksburg?" asked Winston after he had dismissed the uniformed officer.

"Yes."

"And you are sure that the body now at Osterman's Mortuary is that of your sister, Marie Morgan?"

"Positive."

"Have you any idea as to how she came to her death?"

"No. I wish I did have." His long fingers coiled into clenched fists and his eyes, slightly luminous, glinted savagely.

"She was murdered," said Winston quietly, his gaze glued to the other's face. "Strangled to death."

"Who did it?"

"I can't say—just yet. Can you give me any help?"

"No, I'm afraid not."

"Were you present the night of your father's death?"

"No. I was at a military school in the East."

"You were told of the circumstances, of course?"

"Yes. He fell dead just before a dinner in honor of his birthday."

"Exactly. Do you know who were present at that dinner?"

"Yes. Only relatives. Uncles, aunts, cousins."

"And were they all on good terms with your father?"

"No, I can't say that they were. I had heard it said that there was trouble in the family long before, when father and the others were much younger."

"H'm! And what was this trouble about?"

"I don't know. Father never said and I was never with the others. I know he was always very much agitated when he received a letter from one of his brothers or sisters. Mother said once that it was about money. They weren't wealthy like he was and wanted him to divide up with them."

"Was there any reason for this beyond the fact that they wanted his money?"

"No, of course not."

"I judge, then, that your father was not on intimate terms with his relatives?"

"Not at all. He hadn't seen any of them in years until the night of this dinner."

"What could have been his reason for calling them together that way?"

Young Morgan's eyes narrowed with unconscious shrewdness and his hands fluttered nervously.

"I—I don't know," he answered slowly. "There must have been one. Father never did anything without a reason. But I—don't know what it was."

"Do you know how many people were present for this dinner?"

"Yes. Twelve."

"Yet there were thirteen covers laid. Who of the family was missing?"

"Marie, a cousin Joe, likewise in school in the East, and myself."

"Three people but only one vacant place," mused Winston. "You weren't all expected then?"

"None of us three were expected."

"Then who could the other place have been intended for?"

"I don't know." Morgan's tone and manner had grown a little dogged as though he were beginning to resent this close questioning into the personal affairs of his family.

"Why was the table left untouched after your father's sudden death?" snapped Winston suddenly.

Young Morgan suddenly sat up straight and stared directly at his questioner.

"How do you know it was?"

"Because I've seen it," answered Winston simply.

"Well, that's one question I can't answer. It was left for sentimental reasons, I suppose."

"Perhaps. . . . Now, Mr. Morgan, I should like to have a brief outline of the movements of the Morgan family since the Colonel's death."

"I can give you facts concerning only the immediate family."

"Very well."

Morgan hesitated, his brows wrinkled, as he combed the little used corners of his memory.

"As soon as things were settled up we went to Europe. Mother only lived three years. Marie and I stayed on, sometimes separated but more often together. She was studying art and I—I was enjoying myself. Eventually—four years ago, to be exact—I met up with an American who was representing some big American interests in Paris. I joined him, learned the business and when he retired a year ago, took it over.

"About two months ago Marie decided suddenly to return to America. I couldn't get away at the time and she came alone. We communicated regularly until about three weeks since. Then her messages ceased. I cabled four times without any response from her. I deserted everything and came on at once. I couldn't find her but traced her through friends in New York and found she had come on to Ricksburg. I followed at once, arriving here this morning, and found her—at Osterman's."

"H'm! Did your sister have any enemies?"

"Not that I know of."

"She had—er—suitors, I presume," said Winston somewhat hesitantly. "Gentleman friends, at any rate."

"A few, yes. But she wasn't fond of a gay life."

"Were any of them especial rivals?"

"Not that I know of."

"Would you consider insanely jealous love a possible motive for this crime?"

"Possible, yes. But extremely improbable."

"Was your sister in the habit of carrying large sums of money about with her?"

"No."

"Or of wearing valuable jewelry?"

"Never. She possessed only a few pieces and all of them were more unique than valuable."

"Then what could have been the motive for the murder?"

"I'm sure I don't know." His hands clenched again, the long fingers twitching and coiling as though they longed to clasp something.

They lapsed into silence a few moments while Winston's acute brain considered the case carefully from all angles. Young Morgan produced a strange-looking cigarette from a silver case. Winston leaned forward, staring at the round roll.

"Something decidedly different in cigarettes you have there," he said casually.

"Yes. Russian. Learned to like them while I was in Europe. The American brands are almost entirely out of the question over there." He extended the case. "Try one."

Winston accepted but his keen eyes absorbed every detail of the cigarette's appearance before he slowly lifted it to his lips. Slender. Unusually long. The paper and tobacco both decidedly different from that found in American cigarettes. Yet likewise decidedly different from the strange foreign stubs he had found at the Morgan home.

"I should think you'd find it rather difficult to procure these over here," he remarked.

"It's almost impossible, except in the very largest cities. I bought these in Chicago."

"I trust you will pardon these very personal questions," began Winston after a pause. "But you will realize that by virtue of my official position I must make every possible effort to apprehend the person or persons guilty of this crime."

"Of course. And I shall be glad to do everything I can to help you. Ask anything you like."

"Thanks. That simplifies matters. . . . Were your sister's men friends Americans or foreigners?"

"Both. She preferred Americans, of course, but most of them who live in Europe are rather poor specimens. Liquor and so on, you know. So she had quite a few foreign friends. They're persistent devils, too. There's no escaping them."

Winston's eyes flickered with renewed interest.

"Can you give me a concrete example of their persistence?" he asked casually.

"Yes. A good one. Prince Wilhelm Heinrich Adelbert Ratzpfund."

Winston whistled. "Whew! All that tied on one man?"

Morgan smiled slightly. "That's what they called him for short. He had a dozen other names and titles. He looked Swedish to me but he claimed to be an Austrian. Spoke English, French and German with equal facility, so his speech was no indication of his nationality. Anyway, he certainly exhibited dogged persistence in his pursuit of Marie. He was good-looking, evidently cultured and seemed to have enough money so she didn't exactly dislike him. But he insisted on marrying her and she insisted just as stoutly that she was married to her art. So she tried to give him the air, as the saying goes. But there was nothing doing. He followed her relentlessly, not only in Paris where they met but all over Europe—England, Germany, Italy."

"She refused to marry him?"

"Several times."

"Did he seem to resent it?"

"No. Just kept right after her."

"Have you any idea where he is now?"

"No. He left Paris two days after Marie did. He stopped by to see me before he went. Said he was going back to Vienna for a few months."

"H'm! But I suppose you have no actual proof that he did not follow your sister to the United States instead of going on to Vienna?"

"No." Morgan considered that possibility a few moments. "You know, you suggested something logical then. He might have followed Marie over here."

"Was he a hot-headed type of fellow—one who would be likely to kill in a sudden rage?"

"No. He always impressed me as being exactly the opposite, cool and calculating. But of course one never can tell what a man will do when he gets mad."

"No. By the way, what did this chap look like?"

"Tall, well-built fellow. Snappy dresser. A pronounced blonde. Wide blue eyes, fair complexion, yellow mustache and hair. About thirty years old, I imagine."

Winston did not answer. He sat transfixed in his chair, his breathing quick and shallow, his eyes staring straight ahead in the motionless, fixed manner of a man in a trance. For the description which young Morgan had just given him coincided exactly with that of the elusive Mr. Thor Jensen. Could Jensen and Marie's suitor, the Austrian prince, be the same man?

"Had he ever lived in America?" asked Winston finally.

"I don't think so. He hardly ever mentioned it."

"Was he in any sort of business?"

"I don't know positively but I'm sure he wasn't. His time seemed to be his own. Tennis in the morning. Tea at some fashionable place in the afternoon, a theatre or the opera with a couple of hours at some supper club afterward."

"That costs money."

"Yes. He was a liberal spender."

"Incidentally, Mr. Morgan, how did your father make his money?"

"Mining. In the West."

"Gold?"

"Yes."

"He left a rather large estate, I presume?"

"Yes. But not as large as we had anticipated."

"How was it disposed of?"

Morgan hesitated.

"That's a hard question to answer. The terms of the will were rather complicated—"

"I only wished to know the general disposition, not the details."

"In brief, there were trust funds set aside for mother, Marie and I, with further cash payments at stated intervals."

"Did these relatives who were at the dinner receive any?"

"Not a dollar."

"Who got the residue?"

"Er—there wasn't any. The entire estate was disposed of in the will."

"Who drew the will?"

"A local attorney here—Austin J. Barksdale."

"H'm! Well, I guess there's nothing further we can do at the moment, Mr. Morgan. I appreciate very much the information you have given me and I feel sure that you would do anything you could to help me discover your sister's murderer."

"Absolutely."

"Thanks. I may call on you again. Where could I find you?"

"At the St. Giles."

"Very well. Drop in again tomorrow. I may have some news for you."

Winston sat in deep thought for a long time after young Morgan had departed. The interview had furnished him with some startling revelations. His reverie was interrupted by the entrance of his secretary with a telegram. It was from an attorney friend in New York whom he had wired early in the morning:

> *Jensen and Jensen one of largest antique firms here. Junior partner, Mr. Thor Jensen, now in your city.*

17
Raided

Within the next ten minutes Gerard Winston read that telegram a dozen times and after every reading his frown grew deeper and more perplexed. The message upset completely the very plausible theory of the crime which he had evolved after young Morgan's departure.

In the light of that young man's revelations, it certainly was reasonable to conclude that Marie's nobleman suitor from Vienna had pursued her incognito and in a burst of jealous rage murdered her after a final rejection. Such a theory was substantiated by the exactitude with which Morgan's description of Prince Ratzpfund fit the elusive Mr. Thor Jensen. But with the suspect vouched for as Mr. Thor Jensen, a bona fide antique dealer, he hesitated. The unexpected substantiation of Jensen's claims did not fit into Winston's theory at all. In fact, it wrecked it.

Nothing can infuriate any man more than having a pet idea or theory wrecked so Winston set himself to find facts which would prove his version of the crime in spite of the message which was favorable to Jensen. And such facts were easy to find. Would Mr. Thor Jensen, a reliable business man who could prove his identity at once by means of a telegram, have risked the danger and suspicion of escaping from jail if his connection with the case was an entirely honorable one? Not likely. And would outside

people have been on hand to assist in the escape of a legi-
timate business man? Impossible. And what about the initials in his coat? It was unthinkable that Mr. Jensen was
wearing stolen clothes and it was likewise unthinkable
that he was wearing anything but clothes tailor-made to
his measure, which would naturally bear his own initials.
But the fact remained that the initials in Jensen's coat
had not corresponded with his announced name. And what
about the carnation found on the floor of the empty cell,
the same sort of distinctive flower which Winston himself
had found beside the murdered girl's body that strange
night when the whole affair began? Where had it come
from? And who dropped it? Had it been left purposely as
a bit of defiant mockery or left inadvertently by Jensen or
one of his liberators in the rush of escape?

Answers to those questions would not only prove Jensen's real status in the case but would also throw important light on the whole affair. But at the moment it appeared extremely unlikely that he would ever know those
answers. He ground his teeth in sudden rage and struck his
desk with a nervous fist. Damn this mess! One couldn't get
head nor tail of it. The more one worked at it the more
tangled and incomprehensible it seemed to become.

The telephone rang suddenly and he started. He smiled
grimly as he reached for the instrument. His nerves were
growing jumpy under the strain.

"Mr. Winston!" came Grump's voice over the wire and
it was tense with suppressed excitement. "Dodge and that
other fellow who was with him when he followed us in the
taxi have just gone into Barksdale's office."

"All right, thanks. I'll be over at once."

Winston seized his hat and rushed for the building
which contained the office of the mysterious old attorney. And his brain kept pace with the rapid movement of
his body. What could Dodge, the *Beacon* reporter, and his

strange companion Jones want with Barksdale? It must be something in connection with the case in hand.

He found Grump lounging inconspicuously in the lobby of the building where he had a clear view of both the elevators and the stairs.

"They haven't come down yet!" the detective informed him briefly.

"All right. We'll go up."

Winston was surprised and not a little angry to find within himself a strange sinking feeling as the elevator shot upward. It was a feeling of tremendous anticipation, of anxiety, tinged perhaps by just a little fear. But why should he fear Dodge, he demanded of himself? That was the point. Why? It was the uncertainty and his absolute inability to see the reporter's connection with the case that made him regard the man a little anxiously. Uncertainty and suspense were far harder to face calmly than known danger. There was no way to protect one's self against the unknown.

They entered Barksdale's office without knocking. The old attorney looked up quickly at their unceremonious entry but the startled, angry expression on his wizened, satanic countenance gave way to one of forced cordiality as he recognized his visitors.

"Ah yes! Mr. Winston, come in and sit down. I didn't expect to see you so soon!"

But Winston was in no mood for polite pleasantries, forced or otherwise. A quick glance showed him that the other two men were not present. He strode forward to the desk and stood towering over the old attorney, who sat gazing calmly up at him, the corners of his thin-lipped mouth curled into a crafty smile.

"Where are Dodge and Jones?" demanded the district attorney.

"I don't know what you're talking about!" answered Barksdale with calm assurance. His voice held a defiant

tone as if even if he were lying he defied anyone to catch
him at it.

"Come now, Barksdale! Don't try to pull the wool over
my eyes that way!" snapped Winston. "Dodge, the *Beacon* reporter, and another man who says his name is Jones
came up here to your office a few minutes ago. Detective
Grump here saw them."

"I sure did," assented Grump, walking forward, angry
at being made out a liar before his superior. "I saw 'em
come into this very office."

Barksdale surveyed the detective with grimly humorous
gaze.

"Prohibition is an awful thing!" he remarked pleasantly.

Grump bristled under the implication that he had been
drunk and opened his mouth to launch a tirade at the old
man but shut it again abruptly in response to a look from
Winston.

"You're mixed up in this case deeper than I thought!"
remarked the district attorney coldly. "Be careful or you'll
end up in jail along with the rest of them."

"I really don't know what you're talking about!" retorted Barksdale with that bland, irritating calm which he
could effect with such maddening finality. "But I was just
about to telephone your office when you so kindly called.
I have some news for you. My client refuses to become
involved in this case."

Winston's jaw set and his eyes hardened.

"So he refuses to give us any help whatsoever?"

"He is positive that he could give you no help on the
matter with which you think he is connected. The knife
in question has a sentimental value only and he prefers to
lose it rather than be subjected to possible indignities at
the hands of the authorities and to suffer a lot of unpleasant publicity."

"He probably has a very good reason for not wanting to reveal his identity," grunted Winston. "But please inform him for me that *I already know who he is* and that he will be arrested within twenty-four hours if he does not report to my office voluntarily for questioning."

The attorney's jaw sagged a little at that and his brow creased with worry for a moment, then he smiled grimly.

"I shall be glad to give him your message but I don't think it will worry him greatly," he answered with thinly veiled sarcasm.

Winston flushed but he realized that nothing would be gained by losing his temper. So he steeled himself against an outburst and walked out, Grump at his heels.

"Now how in hell did those fellows get out of the building?" demanded the detective as they reached the sidewalk.

"I don't know any more about it than you do," retorted Winston a trifle snappishly. "But I suppose there are other means of leaving the building than the one which we used. I presume Dodge saw you when he and Jones went up. He knew, of course, that you were working on this case with me so he figured that something was up and beat it."

"What did he want up there in the first place?"

"That's what I've been trying to dope out ever since you telephoned me. I can't see the connection between him and Barksdale unless he or Jones is this mysterious client who owns the knife I found in the Morgan library beside that dead girl's body."

"That may be it. You notice that Barksdale had his client's answer to your proposition right after Dodge and Jones had been up there."

"Yes, that's true."

"Either one of them is this client or they're go-betweens."

"Go-betweens, more likely. But we must have them shadowed day and night and find out just exactly what their connection is. . . . Say, Grump, did you notice the ash tray on Barksdale's desk?"

"No. I was too busy trying to keep from batterin' him over the head with something. Why?"

"There were several cigarette stubs in it of high class, cork-tipped Turkish brand, the same sort we found in the ash tray on the sideboard in the Morgan dining-room."

"The hell you say!" exclaimed the detective.

"Absolutely. Now what do you deduce from that?"

"That somebody who smoked that kind of cigarettes had been in Barksdale's office."

"Quite logical," assented Winston dryly. "But who is that somebody?"

"That's what we've got to find out," retorted Grump belligerently.

"I can throw a little light on that matter. Those stubs were not in the ash tray on my first visit to Barksdale's office not much more than an hour ago. Who has visited him since then? Only Dodge and Jones that we know of. And neither one of them is the type of man who would smoke that sort of cigarette."

"Which leaves us in the same condition as the dog who chased his tail," remarked Grump disgustedly. "This is the damnedest puzzle I ever got hold of."

"Well, I'll get back to the office. I'll assign a couple of men to shadow Dodge and Jones. You watch Barksdale's office, remaining as inconspicuous as possible. If anybody you are suspicious of enters the office telephone me. If Barksdale leaves, trail him, then report to me by 'phone."

Gerard Winston struck off down the street at a rapid gait, unaware of the eyes glued to his back from two windows in the building which he had just left.

"Any messages?" asked the district attorney when he reached his office.

"No sir," answered his prim young lady secretary.

"Anybody been in?"

"No sir."

Winston turned and entered his private office, then paused aghast. A second he stood staring at his desk in uncomprehending amazement, then he leaped forward. The neat stacks of papers which he had left on its polished mahogany top were now heaped into one disordered pile, as though they had been gone through, then carelessly thrown aside. Every drawer was open, its contents bulging over its edges from the hasty search. An attempt had been made during his absence to rob him of something which someone considered valuable. Had the unknown succeeded?

18

Jensen Again

Winston made a hurried search of his desk but apparently nothing was missing. What could the unknown intruder have been after? Then suddenly he realized what must have been the object of this daring raid. The knife! He produced it from a trouser pocket and looked at it again. Just a small, very thin, all metal pocketknife. What was there about it that made it so valuable in the eyes of someone? He stared at it earnestly, turning it over and over in his long, well-shaped fingers. There was nothing about it which seemed to offer a clue as to its ownership. It was undoubtedly of foreign make; the grotesque little twin figures stamped on either side of it proving it to be a product of the famous Hinkle Brothers in Germany. Then an idea struck him, an idea so obvious that he was amazed at not having thought of it before—Marie Morgan's suitor, Prince Ratzpfund! The Prince had a German name. Undoubtedly he had been in that country, although perhaps not a native of it. For him to possess a German knife would be quite probable. Had he, after all, followed the girl to America and murdered her in a fit of jealous rage? And was he afraid that this knife would incriminate him? Was this his knife? Was he Barksdale's mysterious client? It was all entirely possible.

Then he thought of Jensen. Jensen was a foreigner, the only one besides the elusive dark man who had appeared in the case so far. In Winston's opinion he was involved deeply, despite the telegram from New York which tended to confirm his announced identity. His escape, evidently effected only with outside assistance, proved that he occupied a larger position in the affair than the casual connection to which he had admitted. This might be his knife. Could he be the guilty man—the murderer? Yes, that was possible. Winston thought again with what exactitude young Morgan's description of his sister's foreign suitor fit the mysterious Jensen. Might Jensen and Prince Ratzpfund be the same man? It was a far-fetched theory yet a possibility. Winston resolved to give it some consideration. In the meantime he would keep the knife on his person. If it were so valuable to someone else it was of equal value to him.

He wondered how the intruder or intruders had gained entrance. His secretary had said there were no visitors during his short absence. And to gain admittance to his private office without her knowledge was an impossibility. Except by the windows. Winston went to them. They overlooked the street and a light layer of grayish dust covered over both sills. Jumbled footprints in this dust proved the manner of the intruder's entrance. An ornamental stone coping ran along the building immediately beneath the windows and a galvanized iron drain pipe above afforded a handhold. The next window to the left was at the end of a public corridor in which the presence of anyone would not excite suspicion. It was quite clear—painfully so.

He turned back to the disordered desk as the telephone rang harshly. It was Grump again. And the detective's voice indicated his tremendous effort at calmness.

"A tall slim dark man has just gone into Barksdale's office," exclaimed the detective. "Answers the description of the man who visited the morgue this morning."

"Arrest him at once!" snapped Winston. "I'll be right over."

He rushed out of the office, disregarding his secretary's questioning look, not even closing the doors behind him. He found Detective Grump standing in the doorway of Barksdale's office, a nonplussed expression on his face.

"Got your man?" demanded the district attorney anxiously.

"No. But I've got some news for you. Barksdale's been murdered."

"Barksdale—murdered!" gasped Winston.

He elbowed Grump to one side and hurried into the office. Barksdale lay sprawled back in his chair, his lean face horribly contorted and quite black.

The body was still warm but it was immediately evident that the lawyer was quite dead. The cause of death was likewise obvious—strangulation. His thin, wrinkled throat still bore the disfiguring marks of strong, ruthless hands while two especially livid spots indicated where murderous thumbs had pressed against his windpipe. One hand, the fingers outstretched tensely, reached toward the paper knife on the desk as though he had made a desperate effort to defend himself.

All the details of the murder corresponded exactly with those of the girl's death at the old Morgan home. Winston felt reasonably certain that both crimes had been committed by the same person. But who? And why?

"I got back here as quick as I could after I 'phoned you," explained Grump, at his elbow. "But Barksdale was dead. The office door was standing wide open."

"Where did you 'phone from?"

"The cigar store downstairs."

"You weren't gone long then?"

"No. Not over five or six minutes."

"H'm! The murderer worked mighty fast. This mysterious strangler exhibits all the skill and deadly certainty of a professional."

"Seems as if we have his identity now, though. Must be that slim, dark man."

"Yes. There was hardly time for him to leave and for anyone else to come in here and commit the crime. But why should he have killed old Barksdale?"

The detective shrugged and both men began a search of the room in an effort to find a motive for this second murder which had been accomplished in the exact manner of the first.

The middle drawer of the steel file in the corner stood half open. Winston shuffled through it, finding a series of heavy paper folders, each with a name on its tab, containing miscellaneous papers and correspondence concerning legal matters. The folders were arranged in alphabetical order and there seemed to be a gap in the midst of the 'M' section. The district attorney's eyes narrowed suddenly and he turned to the desk. One of the file folders, with the name *Morgan* neatly printed in ink on its tab, lay open on the desk, its contents scattered about. He smiled in anticipation and began thumbing through the accumulation of papers.

Most of the papers were old, dated before the death of Colonel Morgan thirteen years before, and dealt with routine business matters which had no special bearing on the case in hand. But there were a few letters dated within the past year and Winston went through these word by word.

"Listen to this, Grump," he said suddenly: "Mr. Thor Jensen, New York City, Dear Sir: Answering your letter of the third instant, wish to say that the information you desire is not in my possession and if it were, I would not give it to you as I can see no reason for your being entitled to it."

"Short and to the point!" commented Grump. "The old boy didn't mince words, did he?"

"No. I wonder what Jensen wanted to know. Ah! here's his letter. Listen to this: Mr. Austin J. Barksdale, Ricksburg, Illinois, Dear Sir: I would greatly appreciate your advising me as to the extent of Miss Marie Morgan's interest in the estate of her father, the late Colonel Morgan, and also the date on which she is to come into the balance of the amount left to her by his will."

"So Jensen was trying to find out about the girl's money?" mused Grump.

"So it seems. And Barksdale wouldn't give him the information he wanted."

Winston stared out the window. These developments confirmed his growing conviction that Thor Jensen and Prince Ratzpfund were one and the same man. He had known of men securing heiresses as wives by pretending to be noblemen then afterwards accepting a comfortable sum from the disillusioned girls to allow them to secure a quiet divorce and go their way without undue publicity or the real facts being revealed.

He found one more letter which he considered of importance. It was to Barksdale from Marie Morgan, dated at Paris three months before, and said that as she had now reached the age of twenty-one she would soon be in Ricksburg in accordance with the instructions of him and Mr. Thornton. Winston replaced the papers in the heavy paper folder, fully satisfied as to the motive for Barksdale's murder. Someone, apparently this slim dark man, whoever he might be, wanted papers and information which were in Barksdale's possession and which the old attorney evidently had refused to relinquish. Barksdale's death had followed and the murderer had helped himself. Winston was positive that important documents, the possession of which might solve the present mystery, had been stolen from that folder by Barksdale's murderer, that they had been the object of the crime.

Winston looked up at a sudden excited shout from Grump to see the elusive Jensen standing in the doorway, a revolver clenched in his right hand, an expression of paralyzed amazement on his handsome countenance. A long moment the men stared at each other, all too surprised to speak or move, then Jensen took a quick shot at Winston and fled.

The district attorney heard the bullet whistle angrily past his ear but he leaped into the hall ahead of Grump. Jensen, not waiting for the elevator, was running for the stairway with the speed of a terrified deer. Winston and the detective both fired but Jensen was pursuing a zig-zag course which made hitting him almost an impossibility. He reached the stairs unscathed and disappeared, the two men not far behind. All the way down, they heard him clattering ahead but they were unable to catch enough of a glimpse of him even to consider the possibility of a shot reaching its mark.

They reached the bottom, flushed and breathless, but Jensen was gone. They spent precious minutes questioning the people who thronged curiously about them but nobody knew anything. Jensen had made good his escape.

"Go back up to Barksdale's office and stay there till I 'phone you," ordered the district attorney crossly.

The detective entered the elevator and Winston hurried back to his own office. He found his secretary fluttering about nervously.

"Oh, Mr. Winston!" she exclaimed excitedly. "Something terrible's happened. Mr. Thornton, the banker, has disappeared. They think he's been kidnapped."

19
Another Note

Gerard Winston deemed Banker Thornton's disappearance of sufficient importance to make a personal investigation. Grump assisted him, after being relieved by a uniformed patrolman whom Winston had sent over for the purpose. Several local officers were already on the scene when Winston and Grump arrived at the bank; but they fell back respectfully at the appearance of the district attorney, allowing him a private conversation with Thornton's secretary, a sad-eyed man with thin gray hair and an air of general depression.

"Mr. Thornton left the bank about three-thirty," explained the secretary. "He telephoned home just before his departure and asked if he should bring anything. Mrs. Thornton mentioned some things she wanted from the drug store and he left. Half an hour later she phoned here and asked if he had gone. I told her he had and she said he had not arrived yet. Shortly after four o'clock a policeman phoned, saying that he had found Mr. Thornton's car parked in the middle of a block which had no houses on either side. He thought perhaps it was stolen but I knew better because Mr. Thornton had left here driving it. I found out from the drug store that he had been there sometime before and gone immediately after making his purchases. I suspected foul play and reported the matter to the police."

"Why did you suspect foul play at once?" demanded Winston.

"Because I knew something was wrong. The location where the car was found was not on Mr. Thornton's way home."

"Were the circumstances your only reason for suspecting foul play?"

"Yes."

"He had no enemies that you know of?"

"No sir, not a one."

"Was he carrying a large sum of money?"

"No sir, I'm positive he wasn't. I got fifty dollars for him just before he left."

"Was he wearing valuable jewelry?"

"No sir. He never wore any at all except his watch and chain."

"You don't think this is a case of robbery, then?"

"No sir. I think he's been kidnapped."

"And why should anyone want to kidnap him?"

"There might be several reasons. He's a very wealthy man. They could hold him for ransom."

"H'm! What are some of the other reasons?"

"Well, he knew a great deal."

"What about?" demanded Winston with interest.

"Many different things—financial matters, of course. He had all sorts of information which would no doubt be of value to other people."

"Can you suggest anyone in particular?"

"No sir."

Winston turned to Grump. "Look the car over," he directed, "then report here to me." He pondered a moment then: "Did Mr. Thornton have any visitors this afternoon?"

"Yes sir, several."

"Were you acquainted with them—that is, were they local people?"

"All except three."

"H'm! Tell me about these three."

"The first was a woman—"

"Describe her."

"She was a brunette, middle-aged, I should judge; well dressed and had the general air of a lady of some importance."

"Do you know her name?"

"No sir. She didn't give it. But she was with Mr. Thornton some time, half an hour or so."

"Do you know what was said during the conference?"

"Most certainly not," answered the secretary with an aggrieved air. "It was in Mr. Thornton's private office and I closed the door from the outside after showing her in."

"Did she seem excited when she left?"

"No, not especially. She looked disappointed, though, and somewhat angry."

"Did Mr. Thornton say anything to you about her?"

"No sir."

"Did he greet her as though he was acquainted with her?"

"Yessir."

Winston halted his examination for a moment. The description the secretary gave exactly fit the description of the woman who had deposited the promised money to his credit in another bank in return for the strange carnation he had found near the girl's body in the Morgan library and which he had unwittingly let slip through his fingers. She had visited Thornton that afternoon. And the banker was acquainted with her. Strange!

"All right," said the district attorney suddenly. "Tell me about the other two visitors. And describe them, please."

"The first was a short, heavy-set man, also middle-aged, and gave the name of Adams—"

"Adams?" demanded Winston, leaning forward, trying to strangle his inward excitement.

"Yes sir."

"Did he have a deep voice?"

"Yes sir."

"H'm!" That must be the man who called the Morgan home the night of the tragedy and asked for Thornton, the man who had been responsible for the telephone at the Morgan home being re-connected and the man who had threateningly advised him not to make any further investigation into the case. Evidently Banker Thornton was the Thornton he had asked for and expected to find there. The trail seemed to be growing hot.

"Did Thornton appear to know this man Adams?"

"I don't know. I didn't see them together. I merely indicated the proper door and Mr. Adams went in."

"Was he with Thornton long?"

"No sir. Not over ten minutes."

"You don't know the purpose or the result of this conference?"

"No, sir, of course not."

"Did Adams appear excited or angry when he left?"

"I didn't notice especially but it is my recollection that he did not."

"All right. What about the third man?"

"He was rather young, tall and slender, and so dark that he looked like a foreigner."

"H'm! Was he smoking?"

"Yes, cigarettes. But they smelled like cigars."

Winston smiled with grim satisfaction. "Very well. Go ahead."

"He refused to give his name but demanded to see Mr. Thornton at once. He said it was very important and I showed him in. It was quite evident that they had never met before. I went out at once, closing the door behind me, but I could frequently hear their voices during the interview that followed."

"Did you hear anything that was said?"

"No sir but I could tell that they were both quite angry."

"Did the conference last long?"

"Not over ten minutes. But it was extremely lively while it lasted. The stranger rushed out suddenly, evidently angry, and Mr. Thornton was in a bad humor all the rest of the afternoon."

"Is there anything further you can tell me?"

"No sir, nothing."

"Very well. Thanks for the information you have given me. I think it will help."

Winston went out in front of the bank to wait for Grump while the officers clustered around Thornton's secretary. They wouldn't get any information of real value, of course, because they didn't know what to ask for. The district attorney now agreed with the secretary that Thornton had been kidnapped. And he suspected that the slender dark man who smoked the strange cigarettes that smelled like cigars was at the bottom of it.

Grump returned shortly. His examination of Thornton's car had revealed nothing of interest save the package of drugs on the floor of the tonneau torn open as though it had been searched. He had found no blood or other sign of violence done.

"The thing was probably carried out peaceably but firmly," observed Winston. "And it might have been done with Thornton's consent, did you ever think of that?"

"No I hadn't— Find out anything here?"

"Yes. Quite a bit. Thornton had three visitors this afternoon—the middle-aged brunette who got the carnation back, the heavy-set deep-voiced man supposed to be J. S. Adams and the tall, slim, dark chap who smokes the funny cigarettes that smell like cigars. He had a stormy session

with the last one, who left in a rage. And I think that's
who kidnapped him."

"Well, what's the conclusion?" demanded Grump impatiently.

"*My* conclusion is that the Morgan estate is at the bottom of this whole affair. Somebody who has no right to it
is trying to get something. And they're not particular as to
means or methods. Marie Morgan has been murdered. The
Morgan attorney has been murdered. The Morgan banker
has been kidnapped—or perhaps murdered, too, for all
we know. This gang—it must be a gang—is after a wad of
money, something big enough to make it worth any sort
of risk."

"All right, logical so far. What's the next step?"

"I have a hunch that something is going to happen out
at the old Morgan place tonight. It seems to be the center of the whole case. I'm going to spend the night there.
Want to go along?"

"Yes."

"All right. Be at my office at ten o'clock."

Grump sauntered away, his face bearing an expression
that was not exactly enthusiastic. Winston smiled grimly
at the detective's evident anxiety regarding things beyond
his understanding and returned to his office.

His secretary had gone but a note lay on his desk. It
bore neither stamp nor address, indicating that it had not
been sent through the mail, but the handwriting of the
simple legend: *Mr. Gerard Winston,* gave him a shock. With
trembling fingers he tore open the envelope and extracted
the single sheet of paper. His eyes widened in amazement
as he read: *Please meet me in the library of the old Morgan
home tonight at midnight. Marie.*

He examined the handwriting closely. It seemed to be
the same hand as that in which those first notes had been
written. But of course that was an absolute impossibility.

Marie was dead, murdered. This note must be a forgery, a ruse to get him out to the old Morgan home. Perhaps they intended to murder him. It was more than likely. But he felt that the mystery could be cleared up only through that old house. He had decided to spend the night there. Nothing could alter his decision.

20

Strange Happenings

Ten o'clock that night found Gerard Winston and Detective Grump well out on the road which led past the old Morgan home. They were ahead of schedule but Winston had always believed that he had been a contributing cause to Marie's murder by being late for the appointment which she had pleaded with him to keep. So he intended to be there well ahead of time tonight.

He had phoned his secretary at home to ascertain the method of the note's delivery. It had been brought by a messenger boy of the local telegraph service. He had tried to find the boy who delivered it in order to question him as to who had hired him but none would admit having visited his office that afternoon. It looked like bribery. And his secretary had been unable to give a description of the boy which would assure identification.

"I tell you, Winston, I don't like this business tonight," said Grump over the hum of the running car.

"I don't exactly *like* it myself, old timer," admitted the district attorney. "But duty and pleasure are usually two different things. The little expedition is duty. And I believe it's going to bear fruit. Somebody had a very definite purpose in sending me that note."

"Evidently," agreed the detective grimly. "They probably want a good chance to bump you off."

"You may be right. But they'll have to be mighty quick on the trigger if they do. I'm well armed and I don't intend to take any chances."

"Better not. There's a lot more behind this than we know yet and it's been proved that whoever it is isn't a bit squeamish about such a slight matter as a murder or two."

"You're not afraid of a ghost getting you, are you?" asked Winston with a laugh.

"Hell no! If it is a ghost it can't get me and if it isn't I'll take my chances of getting it first."

The young district attorney chuckled to himself. The words and tone were both very brave but he knew that the most heroic of men were thoroughly frightened by things beyond their understanding. They lapsed into silence, the only sound the steady, rhythmic purr of the powerful car as they shot along the smooth road. But Winston was doing a lot of thinking and he imagined Grump was. No trace had been found of the missing Banker Thornton. Nor had any clues as to the identity of Barksdale's murderer been discovered. The detectives he had set on the trail of Dodge, the reporter, and his mysterious friend Jones, had reported complete inability to find out their whereabouts. The whole affair seemed hourly to grow more tangled and incomprehensible.

They drove the last quarter mile in complete darkness to prevent warning possible enemies at the Morgan place of their approach. Winston brought the machine gradually to a complete stop as they reached the boundary of the estate.

"Better leave the car outside," counseled Grump.

"No," objected Winston. "It would attract attention if anyone should come along. And remember that there isn't another like it around Ricksburg. They would know who had dropped in for a call before they ever reached the house. We'll hide it among the shrubbery inside the grounds."

Cautiously he turned in through the big wide gate, which was still open, up the graveled driveway perhaps twenty yards, then turned sharply off to the left as he noticed an opening in the undergrowth. When they returned to the driveway afoot they looked back for the car but it was completely hidden in the darkness by the wilderness of trees and bushes. Then they walked resolutely toward the house, carefully keeping to the grassy edge of the drive so that their shoes would not crunch in the gravel.

Like twin ghosts, but vague blurs against the uncertain shadows of the grounds, they stole toward the weird old house. So far as they could tell it was completely enveloped in darkness. And they noticed for the first time how intense the blackness was. There was no sign of a moon to lighten the somber blackness of the sky, a blackness which was so unrelieved and impenetrable that they could not see the outline of the strange round tower and the chimneys against the sky. And they were thankful for it. Even an expert shot was more than likely to miss in such total darkness.

They reached the steps without incident and started up slowly, Winston in the lead, testing each step cautiously with outstretched foot for warning creaks before placing his full weight upon it. The door was closed but it opened readily to Winston's touch, revealing a repellant dark void beyond. There was no light anywhere and Winston refused to reveal their presence by using one. Cautiously he led Grump to what he believed was the location of the doorway that opened into the library.

His hand found the jamb and penetrated beyond. The door was open and they entered hesitantly, fearful of falling over stray furniture. Then Winston closed the door and depressed the button of his flashlight. They were in the library. And apparently it had not been touched since their last visit when they had searched for the missing policemen. The huge heap of books lay exactly as they had before. And then the long yellow beam revealed something new. On either side of the room lay a new heap of books, all as carelessly thrown aside as the others. Not a book remained on the many shelves.

"Hunting for something," growled Grump in a low tone. "Must be valuable."

"Evidently, from the effort they've made to find it. About all you could hide in a book would be a paper of some sort."

"Unless it was something written on a page."

"Possible but not probable. They wouldn't be hunting for something written inside the covers of these books. This looks to me as though they were hunting a paper which they suspected was hidden inside the covers of some volume in this library."

"Wonder if there's anybody else in the house now," remarked Grump and his voice held a trace of nervousness.

"Can't say—" Winston's voice trailed off into paralyzed silence and he felt Grump grasp his arm in a grip so tight that it hurt. From somewhere came those phantom footsteps again, slow and solemn, as though someone were climbing stairs with a great effort. It was inexpressibly terrifying.

"Good God!" gasped Grump hoarsely.

With the first sound of the phantom footsteps Winston had snapped off his flashlight, throwing the room into sudden and complete darkness again. Now he left Grump and moved to the wall which must separate the room from that mysterious tower into which it seemed impossible to gain entrance. He could hear the footsteps much more clearly. Evidently they were of human instead of supernatural origin. But the sound was not even in volume. It diminished and grew stronger, diminished and grew stronger, as if the climber might be ascending a circular stairway. But with every cycle it was less noticeable until it finally was no longer audible.

"Those footsteps were human, Grump," said Winston in a low tone, rejoining the detective.

"I hope so," answered the officer in a tone which suggested a sinking sensation somewhere around the wishbone and cold perspiration on the forehead.

"A ghost, even an experienced one, simply could not make sounds as realistic as that," continued Winston positively. "That was someone in the tower and he was walking upstairs, a circular iron stairway, as near as I could tell."

"Must have been an old man."

"Yes. Or a fat man with a bad heart. He was taking his time, all right."

"But how'd he get in there? We've searched the house from top to bottom and can't find an entrance."

"I know. But there must be one. It's just well concealed, that's all."

Well, let's try to find it," answered Grump nervously. "When people are walkin' so close to me that I can hear 'em I want to see 'em, too. At least, I want to know they *can* be seen."

Winston chuckled at the detective's evident fear of the supernatural.

"Well, I'll bet this chap could be seen all right if we could get inside that tower. Ghosts are supposed to float around with an occasional sound of clanking chains, you know."

"Brrr!" said Grump and Winston could imagine the involuntary shiver that accompanied the sound.

Their second search for an entrance to the tower commenced in the library. In the next half hour they covered with extreme care every inch of its walls. But they gained nothing except a sweat and rather snappish tempers.

"There's no entrance from this room," admitted Grump finally.

"If there is we are unable to find it," corrected Winston, exhibiting the lawyer's penchant for exactness in statement.

"Have it your own way! At any rate, we can't get into the tower. There are three other places where we can look for the entrance with a reasonable hope for finding it—the cellar, the second floor and the attic."

"Correct," agreed the district attorney ironically. "What would you advise?"

"Examining all three at once," retorted Grump sharply.

"If we do, we're sure to reveal our presence here."

"Can't help it," answered the detective doggedly. "I think this whole mystery is centered in that damned tower and I want to know what's in it."

"So do I. But I'm more interested in knowing the identity of the people who are involved in this thing."

"Well, you're the boss! Handle it to suit yourself!" Grump lit a cigarette and the flaring match revealed his face set in an expression which might be classified as disgusted.

"I'm going to act on your suggestion," assented Winston finally. "We'll get to the second floor as quietly and as quickly as possible then shut ourselves in the room corresponding to this one and see if we can find the entrance there."

Winston opened the door and they moved cautiously out into the great dark hall. It was cold and damp like a tomb. Winston even found himself inclined to shiver as the atmosphere of the old place permeated his being. But with light in one hand and pistol in the other, both ready for instant use, he resolutely led the way to the stairs. Then Grump caught his arm again in that viselike grip which was a habit of his when excited. And Winston stared—at a vague white blur apparently halfway up the stairway. Suddenly it moved, then rushed ceilingward but without a sound. Practical though he was, Winston found himself breathing fast and hard, almost with difficulty. And there was a lump in his throat that he couldn't dislodge.

With sudden resolve he took the risk and snapped on his flashlight. Its beam fluttered an instant, then settled full on the running figure of a girl dressed in white. Winston recognized the apparition instantly as that which had given him such a turn two nights before while so far as he knew the body lay in the library. It was all the more awful and inexplicable now for they both knew for a positive fact that Marie Morgan's body lay in Osterman's Mortuary back in Ricksburg. The thing vanished at the top of the stairs. Grump's breath rattled noisily in his constricted throat and his eyes were terrible when he turned to stare at Winston.

"Come on!" snapped the district attorney and leaped up the stairs.

He didn't wait to see whether or not the detective was following but ascended with the powerful leaps of a mountain goat, his light focused on the spot where the apparition had vanished. But he found only emptiness and silence, the only sound the echo of his own progress. Grump joined him, wild-eyed and panting, more, Winston felt, from the fear of being left alone in the dark in the weird old mansion than from any desire to help in a search for the apparition which had just fled from them. But he assisted his superior willingly enough in the thorough combing of the second floor which followed. But no trace of the person or ghost or whatever it was could be found. Grump held to the belief that the thing was supernatural manifestation and his face showed it. Winston didn't know what to think. But he realized that his breathing and heart action were still far from normal.

From an upper window they saw a small, hazy light moving about the grounds in an erratic course but in the general direction of the house.

"That's worth investigating," commented Winston.

They returned to the first floor quietly and in darkness. The light was approaching the house more directly
now and with greater speed. It reached the steps that led
up to the porch and through the dirty windows they could
see that it was a flashlight in the hand of a man about
which nothing could be distinguished save the vague out-
lines of his figure.

He hesitated a moment, then came up the steps slowly
and with evident caution. Winston and Grump stationed
themselves on either side of the wide door and waited.
Both were trembling with anticipation.

21

Valuable Clues

The door opened slowly and a black bulk stood outlined against the darkness. A moment the man stood there, then advanced a step or two into the hallway. Winston kicked the door shut and snapped on his light. It revealed Detective Grump, his face set in a ferocious expression, pointing his revolver at the middle coat button of Doctor Sherwood.

"H'm! So we meet again!" exclaimed Winston.

"Yes—if you say so," assented the young doctor, his eyes blinking in the glare of the sudden illumination. "But I can't see you behind that light and I'm sorry to say I can't place your voice."

"You can't?" said the district attorney, slightly sarcastic. "That's strange. We met only night before last, out there on the porch."

"Oh yes, now I place you. You're the mysterious man who refused to reveal his identity and this"—pointing to Grump—"is the gentleman who was kind enough to escort me to my car, no doubt to secure its license number."

"Quite correct," admitted Winston dryly. "And now please walk into the library. I want to have a talk with you." Unhesitatingly Sherwood walked to the library door and entered the room beyond. Winston and Grump followed. And on the district attorney's face, largely hidden

by the darkness, was an expression of grim triumph. He
closed the door then focused the light full on the young
doctor's countenance.

"You have quite a bit to explain, doctor. I have suspected right along that you had a much greater connection
with this affair than you admitted the other night. And
now I know it. Just now you came straight to the library
without my indicating its location. Which proves that you
are acquainted with the house from past visits. When were
you inside this house before and what was your reason for
being here?"

The veiled accusation did not disconcert Doctor Sherwood in the least. He smiled ruefully at the unconscious slip
he had made but his gaze did not waver. He exhibited none
of the symptoms of a guilty man confronted with his crime.

"Perhaps I'd better tell you the whole story," he answered calmly.

"By all means," assented the district attorney. "But
please confine it to the absolute truth. At the moment, I
have neither time nor inclination for fiction, interesting
as it might be."

"Very well. But first I must know your identity. I must
have it proven to me that you are entitled to know of my
part in this affair, that my information is going into the
proper hands."

"I am Gerard Winston, the district attorney."

"Can you prove it?"

"I can."

From his inside coat pocket Winston produced half a
dozen letters bearing his name and passed them over. Sherwood shuffled through them slowly, carefully, without the
slightest hint of nervousness. Then he returned them with
a smile.

"Very well," he said calmly. "You're vouched for, all
right. Now I'll tell you what I know about this. I intended

to come to your office anyway tomorrow morning as I felt that the information I possess would be of some value to you."

"Is it a long story?"

"Rather."

"Then we may as well sit down."

The three men dropped into chairs and Sherwood lit a cigarette with small, slender-fingered hands that were rock-steady.

"I am a specialist in plastic surgery," began the doctor, "an associate of the famous specialist, Rubinski, formerly of Vienna but now of Chicago. About two months ago a young woman was brought to me for an operation. A man accompanied her. She was already quite pretty but she wished to be made more so. When I inquired just what changes she wished made the man produced a photograph of a beautiful young woman and they both said she wanted to be made to look as exactly as possible like that picture. I told them I thought I could accomplish the desired objective and we agreed on a fee of twenty-five hundred dollars, one thousand of which the man paid in cash on the spot.

"I performed the operation and arranged for her to remain in seclusion in a small private sanitarium in order to let time and nature obliterate the scars as much as possible. They insisted that the affair be given no publicity and from what they said to me and to each other I gathered the impression that the girl was doing motion picture work and wanted her face changed so that it would screen better.

"In due time, the operation a complete success, I allowed her to leave the sanitarium and the man paid me the balance of the agreed fee. But during the association I had become rather fond of the girl. She was a charming creature and now quite beautiful. I called on her several

times at the home of her aunt where she was visiting. At
first I was somewhat diffident, thinking that the man who
had accompanied her might have a place in her heart but
it was soon evident that he did not. He never visited her
at the aunt's home. In fact, she cautioned me several times
not to mention him in front of her aunt and was especially
vehement about not mentioning the operation to her aunt.
I gathered that she was going on the screen in opposition
to the wishes of her relatives and of course I could understand her reasons for not wanting the operation made
public, so I was known to her aunt only as a friend."

"Did you find out the names of these various people?"
asked Winston tensely.

"Of course. But I think it would be better if I tell my
story in my own way. Then I will answer any questions you
care to ask."

"Very well. Go ahead."

"About a week ago she told me that she had to come
out to Ricksburg for a few days 'on business.' I—er—proposed before she left but she rejected me, saying that it
was impossible, though she refused to say why. She was
tearful and somewhat hysterical about it, I questioned her
at great length but she refused to tell me anything more.

"The day after she left I thought of the man who had
accompanied her to my office. I was suspicious of him and
of his connection with her. She had said nothing more to
me about the film proposition and I began wondering who
he was. Jealousy is a powerful thing, you know, and I became convinced in my own mind that she was involved in
some sort of an affair with him from which she could not
escape. I went to her aunt and told her the whole story.
She became highly excited, though she refused to say why,
and when I suggested coming to Ricksburg insisted on
coming with me. Which she did.

"The day the girl left I gave her a bouquet of carnations—"

"Were they a new kind which are scarce and quite expensive?" demanded Winston, unable to contain himself any longer.

"They were. She wore four or five of them pinned to her coat when she left and the aunt did likewise when we departed. When we arrived here day before yesterday we were unable to find the girl and finally came here to search for her."

"And why did you think she might be here?"

"Because her name was Marie Morgan."

Two gasps split the tense silence like pistol shots.

"Marie Morgan!" exclaimed Winston.

"Yes. Her aunt said she was a daughter of the old Colonel Morgan who formerly owned this place. As I was saying, we came here to search for her but did not find her. We were here in the evening, about six or seven o'clock. When we returned to my brother's home, where the girl's aunt is staying, she found that she had lost one of the carnations.

"The next morning the paper told of a girl being murdered here the night before. I visited Osterman's Mortuary and found that the body was that of Marie. And immediately the aunt became highly excited because of the lost carnation. She felt sure the thing would be found by the authorities who, were they so inclined, would find it a simple matter to trace the flower because of its unusualness, thus directing suspicion against her and me. She had a horror of being involved in the case and I didn't exactly care for it myself—my name in the papers in connection with a girl's murder couldn't possibly do me any good, professionally or otherwise.

"She insisted on writing you a note, offering a handsome reward for the flower. I counseled against that on the grounds that such procedure would merely focus your attention on the flower, which you might not have noticed before, but she insisted and I helped her get it back. I worked out the little scheme which proved successful and waited in the vacant house until you deposited the flower in the mailbox."

"Then this aunt is the mysterious 'X'?" queried Winston sharply.

"Yes."

"She is a large brunette of middle age?"

"Yes."

"What's her name?"

"Mrs. Grant."

"H'm! Go ahead."

"That's all," concluded Doctor Sherwood. "Now ask any questions you like. I shall be glad to answer them."

"This Mrs. Grant must be in good circumstances."

"She is."

"What is her relationship to the Morgans?"

"She is a sister of the Colonel Morgan who owned this place."

"Who was this man that accompanied the girl to your office?"

"He gave the name of Arthur Preston but Marie called him Tony."

"Describe him."

"He is a tall, slender, handsome chap, about thirty years of age, I imagine, a fancy dresser, and with a swarthy complexion."

"A swarthy complexion, eh? Does he smoke long, brown paper Cuban cigarettes which smell like cigars?"

"He does."

"Ah!" Winston's sudden exhalation was triumphant and he glanced significantly at Grump, whose breath was coming in quick gasps. Now they were beginning to get somewhere. "Do you think you did a good job in making Marie look like this photograph?"

"I flatter myself that I did a very good job indeed. I don't believe anyone could have told them apart."

"Could you identify this girl without a possibility of mistake?"

"Yes."

"How?"

"By various tiny little scars which would not be seen or noticed by other people."

"Did you see these scars on the body at Osterman's?"

"I did."

"Then that girl who was murdered in this very room night before last is the girl you operated on?"

"Positively."

"H'm," mused Winston. "Well, doctor, you have given me quite a bit of help but I'm still somewhat at sea for a solution of the case. Have you anything to suggest?"

"I'm sorry to say I haven't."

"Did Marie ever say anything to you about the Morgan estate?"

"No."

"She never said who or what this man Preston was?"

"No."

"Do you know anything about the tower on this house?"

"I didn't know it had one. I was only inside here once before, you know, and when I came back later that night on the chance that I might learn something you gentlemen ran me away immediately."

"Do you know Dodge, the reporter for the morning *Beacon?*"

"I don't know anyone here except my brother and his wife."

"Why did you come back here tonight?"

"In an effort to find out something about this mysterious affair. As you can imagine, I felt mighty vindictive about the men who murdered Marie and I was anxious to find out something which would bring them to justice."

"Yes, naturally. Well, it's a strange mix-up and we're not to the bottom of it yet."

22
The Closed Tower

Winston got up and paced about the confines of the library. At last he went to the door and opened it. A draught of cold air swept past his face. An outside door was open somewhere. Then his ears caught the sound of a person moving around to the rear. Throwing caution to the winds he hurried back through the long dark hall, moving as cautiously, as was consistent with speed, light and revolver ready.

At the dining room door he paused. He could hear no sound but he could feel the presence of a person nearby. He gritted his teeth and pressed the button of his flashlight. Its beam, hurtling through the intense darkness, centered full upon a figure near the sideboard—young Morgan. There was a revolver clenched tightly in his right hand and he swung it in the direction of the light as its glow made him blink.

"It's all right, Morgan," called Winston quickly. "This is District Attorney Winston."

Relief flashed into the young man's face and he dropped the gun into his pocket as he advanced.

"What are you doing here?" he asked.

"I might ask you the same question." Winston's tone was pleasant but the remark was nevertheless a demand.

"I was hopeful that I might find something out here—a clue to the people who—murdered Marie."

"I'm out here for the same purpose. And I hope we shall be successful before the night is over."

He didn't mention the matter of the last note signed Marie and written apparently in the same handwriting as the others. It would be unkind to raise false hopes which later might be dashed.

"Why? Have you found some new clues?" asked young Morgan anxiously.

"Yes. Several. And I have a lot of questions to ask you. Did your sister ever have a plastic surgery operation performed on her face?"

"Not that I know of."

"Have you ever heard of a Doctor Sherwood?"

"No."

"Was your sister acquainted with a tall, slender, dark man who smokes brown paper Cuban cigarettes that smell like cigars, whose name is Arthur Preston but whom she called Tony?"

"Not to my knowledge."

Morgan was plainly at a loss to account for the questions. It was evident that his answers were truthful. Winston broached another subject.

"Have you an aunt in Chicago?"

"Yes."

"Tell me all about her."

"Well, there isn't much to tell. She is a widow named Mrs. Grant, a sister of my father."

"Was she mentioned in your father's will?"

"No. But she is quite comfortable. Her husband left her in good circumstances."

"What was her feeling about being left out of the will?"

"She was quite vindictive about it. But she was mad at father before that, we never knew why."

"Were you and your sister friendly with her?"

"Yes. We both visited her several times and she was always nice to us."

"Had your sister visited her recently?"

"Not that I know of."

"Give me a description of her, please."

"She is a brunette of rather ample figure, somewhere around fifty years old, I imagine."

"H'm! Has she been in Ricksburg recently?"

"I don't think so. To my knowledge, her last visit here was the night of my father's birthday dinner, before which he died."

Winston paused to think. This aunt and her hatred of old Colonel Morgan injected a new element into the case. The district attorney considered it carefully from all angles. Was it possible that Mrs. Grant had transferred that enmity for the old Colonel to his children?

"Did this aunt bear any ill-feeling toward your sister?"

"Absolutely not. I'm positive she didn't. There was no reason why she should have."

Winston considered a moment then introduced another topic—the one which was uppermost in his mind.

"How do you get into the tower?" he demanded suddenly.

"What tower?" Morgan's puzzlement was obvious.

"The tower that is on the corner of this house. Surely you've noticed it."

"Yes, I recall it, now that you mention it. But I was around here but little after I reached the age of thirteen and a child takes the various things about his home for granted, you know. I've never paid any attention to it."

"Well, it's worth noticing. In fact, I consider it the key to this whole mysterious affair."

"You do? Why?"

"There are several reasons. First, the rooms which adjoin this tower do not conform to its shape, proving that its space is unaccounted for. Second, I have twice heard footsteps in this house when it was impossible to see anyone. On the first occasion I was unable to locate them but tonight I heard them distinctly coming from beyond the library wall. The tower adjoins the library, which proves that the walker was in the tower."

"Looks that way," admitted young Morgan. "But how could it be the center of this affair?"

"I think it contains something which this gang is after."

"That's possible. Might be something extremely valuable, too. Father always was a little eccentric and the estate was much smaller than we expected."

"What do you say we try to find our way into the tower?"

"I'm game. Where do we start?"

"I was in hope you would be able to furnish that information."

"I'm sorry to say I can't. But I'll be glad to help in any way possible."

"Fair enough. Was there any room in the house where your father spent a great deal of time?"

"There were two—the library and his bedroom. He often locked himself into one or the other for two or three hours at a time."

"H'm! There may be an entrance into the tower from the library but I don't think so. At least I haven't been able to find it and I've gone over the room with a fine-tooth comb, as the saying goes. Let's try the bedroom."

"All right. It's on the second floor, directly above the library."

"Fine. Just a minute until I go back to the library. A couple of my men are there and I want to tell them to wait for me."

"Why not take 'em along?"

"The more people, the more noise. And we don't want to advertise our presence any more than necessary. Silence is golden here tonight."

"Very well."

Winston returned to the library. Sherwood and Grump sat opposite each other in impassive silence in the big dark room, their faces ghastly in the glow of the latter's flashlight.

"You fellows stay here a few minutes," directed Winston. "I'm going to hunt an entrance to the tower."

Grump leaped to his feet.

"But you shouldn't go exploring around this old place alone," he objected.

"I'm not going alone," answered his superior calmly.

Grump stared. His overpowering curiosity was evident but Winston chose not to appease it. With only a smile in the detective's direction he left the room, closing the door behind him, and rejoined young Morgan. Together, silently and with careful step, they ascended the broad stairs up which Winston had pursued that apparition of the fleeing girl not long before. But nothing unusual happened.

They reached the second floor and Morgan led the way to his father's bedroom. Then they locked themselves in and set to work. Like all the other rooms in the house, it was enormous and furnished in a top-heavy manner with massive carved walnut pieces of old-fashioned design which would have brought a pretty penny as antiques. Winston's eyes sparkled as he noted the paneled walls. To conceal a secret door in a paneled wall was a simple matter. But finding it was another matter. Or so it proved to be in this case. Half an hour's intensive effort availed them absolutely nothing in the way of discovering an entrance to the closed tower.

"That's provoking!" growled young Morgan.

"Rather," assented Winston, mopping his perspiring face. "But we're not through yet. Let's see if we can move this bed."

They both laid hold of the huge canopied bed and prepared to exert all their strength to move it. To their intense surprise it swung about easily. Either of them could have moved it with one hand. Winston leaped to that section of the wall which had been protected by the head. Quickly his hands ran over the paneling, pressing every inch of it. With startling suddenness a section almost as large as a door swung inward, revealing a repellantly dark void. Winston stepped through and Morgan followed. They found themselves on a sort of landing with an iron stairway extending both above and below in a long easy circle.

"Shall we go up or down?" whispered young Morgan.

"Might as well start at the bottom and work up," answered Winston and started down the stairs with the other at his heels.

The stairway descended in a sort of passage, not more than three feet wide, bounded on either side by rough brick walls. It terminated at a patch of cement floor beyond which was an iron door partly open. Winston found his breath coming and going unpleasantly fast as he pushed the door wide open and crossed the threshold behind the protecting glare from his flashlight. Morgan crowded forward almost on top of him in his anxiety to penetrate the secret of the tower.

They were in a circular room, some twelve feet in diameter, piled high with small packing cases which looked to be extremely strong. They were of some fine-grained, well-seasoned dark wood, stoutly put together with screws and bound with strips of iron. One lay in the center of the floor with a part of its lid missing. Its contents, which came even with the top as if the box had been made to fit, gleamed dull yellow in the rays of the electric torch. Winston reached in to pick up one of the bars. Its weight was an obvious shock to him for he paused to take a better grip before lifting it. Together, he and young Morgan studied the object, a solid, oblong shape some four by ten inches and an inch thick.

"A gold ingot!" exclaimed young Morgan.

"Yes. And this box is filled with them. All these other boxes must be filled with them. Why, there's millions here!"

"Evidently!" agreed the other dryly. "No wonder father's estate was small."

23
Captives

Winston dropped the piece of gold back into the box where it landed with a dull clang.

"It would have been a good joke if you had sold this old place," he remarked with grim humor.

"We couldn't. That was in the will."

"What was the provision regarding it?" asked the district attorney casually, making an effort to mask his deep interest.

Morgan frowned and hesitated.

"Oh, well, I might as well tell you about it," he said finally. "Maybe it will help clear up this affair. There was a paragraph in father's will directing that this house and all its contents were to be held in trust until March of this year."

"H'm! That's about two months ago. And who was the beneficiary of this provision?"

"The thirteenth guest."

"The thirteenth guest?" exclaimed Winston.

"Yes. You may remember that the table was set for thirteen at that fatal birthday dinner of my father's. The places are still there. I was looking at them when you discovered me. But only twelve people were present. Just before he was stricken he proposed a toast to *'the thirteenth guest'!*"

"Do you know the identity of this mysterious thirteenth guest?"

"No."

"Do you know anyone who does?"

"No."

"Who held this property in trust?"

"Father's banker here."

"Thornton?"

"Yes."

"H'm! Wouldn't he be likely to know the identity of the person he was to deliver this property to eventually?"

"That's right. He would. He'd have to! I hadn't thought of that before."

"Thornton disappeared this afternoon on his way home. His car was found abandoned in a lonely spot. The supposition is that he was kidnapped. Do you see the connection?"

"Do I? Well, rather!"

"And now you can see my reason for coming here tonight. I felt that Thornton was kidnapped to enable this gang to question him at leisure, perhaps to torture him, in order to make him divulge information which they wanted. Evidently they found out about this valuable cache in some way. Undoubtedly they will secure the desired information—it's easy to accomplish a purpose when you don't mind what means you use—and I believe they will act on it tonight."

"Wouldn't be surprised. And if they do, bullets are going to fly."

"Right," assented Winston grimly. "And a good many of 'em will probably be flying at us. But it's up to us to give a good account of ourselves."

There was nothing more that could be done in the treasure room at the moment and they decided to ascend in a continuation of their tour of exploration. Around and around they climbed the circular iron stairs and Winston

wondered grimly what Grump and Sherwood, seated beyond the wall in the library, would think of the eerie footsteps.

Just beyond the landing they came upon another iron
door but this one was closed with a heavy bolt. Winston
put his ear to the crack. He could hear strange sounds as
if something were being dragged across the floor. Immediately his mind reverted to those awful moments when
he and Grump had first heard those phantom footsteps
in the wall, when they had been accompanied by that low
slithering rumble. Savagely he got a grip on his nerves and
reached for the bolt. It slid back in its rusty track with
an agonized screech. Then he kicked the door open and
shot his light into the dark void beyond. The long yellow
beam made a nervous circle of a round room apparently
the exact counterpart of the treasure room below, then
came to rest on three ominously quiet figures stretched
out on the hard floor. All were gagged and tightly bound
hand and foot. Winston advanced into the room, Morgan
crowding close on his heels, and stared at the three inert
heaps. Then he recognized them as Murphy, Harrison and
Thornton.

Within two minutes all were released but they were
unable to rise because of their stiffened limbs. But their
tongues were far from useless. All three babbled an incoherent stream of indignant profanity. Even staid Banker
Thornton put in a few well-chosen words about his cap-
tors.

"Wait a minute! Wait a minute!" commanded Winston.
"Let's have this thing in chronological order. Murphy, you
and Harrison disappeared first. Tell your story!"

"There isn't much to tell," snapped the burly Murphy.
"We was a-settin' in the library smokin' when a part of the
wall flew out and—"

"A part of the wall flew out!" exclaimed Winston.

"Yes it did!" retorted Murphy belligerently, all the deference knocked out of him by the indignities he had suffered. "And don't say it didn't, neither, because Harrison and me both seen it and we hadn't had a drop of nothin' except water. . . . As I was sayin', a part of the wall flew out and somebody behind it started shootin'. We got behind them heavy chairs—they was as good as a cement wall—and shot back. Then somebody started shootin' from the doorway behind us. So we had two of 'em to fight. But we done our best until our cartridges run out. One of the devils hit me in the arm. Then the man behind us threw a big bottle into the room and shut the door. He evidently throwed it a-purpose because it hit the table and broke. It was full of somep'n' that smelled like a drug store hit by a cyclone and the first thing you know Harrison and me didn't know nothin'. When we woke up, here we was, trussed up like a couple of chickens ready for the oven."

In spite of the tenseness of the moment Morgan laughed at the comical recital, which was accompanied by illustrative gestures made possible by the blood flowing through Murphy's arms again, and even Winston smiled.

"That's all you know, then?"

"Yes. And for God's sake, gimme somep'n' to smoke."

Morgan passed around cigarettes while Winston turned to Banker Thornton who was purple in the face from rage, and spluttering incoherent but dire threats against certain "damnable ruffians" that he "hoped rotted in jail."

"Calm down now, Mr. Thornton, and tell me all about it," advised Winston soothingly.

"Calm, *hell!*" exploded the old banker. "Do you realize what you're asking, my dear sir? I've been kidnapped, beaten, *tortured.*" His voice rose to a shriek at the last word. "And you ask me to be calm." He snorted savagely.

"Well, I can't do anything for you until you tell me what happened."

Winston lighted a cigar then stared at the irate old banker with irritating calmness.

"What do you want to know?" growled Thornton finally.

"Everything—all that has happened since you disappeared this afternoon."

"I was kidnapped on the way home. Three ruffians jammed me into the curb on Lawndale avenue near Twenty-seventh street. I thought it was a hold-up at first but two of them climbed into my car and with drawn revolvers commanded me to drive to a lonely spot. Then they forced me into their car and brought me here. Two other men were in the library—"

"Describe them please?"

"One was dark and the other was a decided blonde. Both were tall, good-looking young men, well-dressed."

"Did the dark one smoke brown paper cigarettes that smelled like cigars?"

"Yes. He looked like a foreigner of some sort. The other fellow called him Tony. They questioned me at length but—"

"Their questions concerned the Morgan estate?"

"Yes."

"And especially, the means of entering this tower?"

"Yes. But I refused to answer. They threatened me with revolvers but I wasn't afraid for I realized that they wouldn't kill 'the goose that might lay the golden egg.' But they beat me unmercifully with sections of rubber hose. And still I wouldn't talk. I felt that they had done their worst but I underestimated both their resourcefulness and their cruelty. They heated irons and put to my feet. I couldn't stand that. In a frenzy from pain, I told them everything. Then they found their way into the tower and brought me here."

"Well, you have had a hot time," exclaimed Winston sympathetically. "No wonder you want those fellows brought to justice. And I'm just as anxious as you are. Where are they now?"

"I don't know. But they said they were going to town for a truck to haul the gold away."

"Then that's probably the reason why we haven't encountered them so far tonight. But no doubt we shall meet later . . . Incidentally, Mr. Thornton, there are a few questions I want to ask you while, we're here together."

"Well?" growled the old banker, looking up suspiciously.

"Who is the thirteenth guest?" demanded Winston, making heroic efforts to keep his voice calm.

Thornton's jaws snapped shut with stubborn determination.

"These crooks already have a great deal of information more than is good for us," continued the district attorney seriously. "To combat them successfully and apprehend them I must know every detail of this affair, past and present. I can hail you into court tomorrow and make you talk but you will help things along and perhaps assure the victory of justice by talking *now* and answering my questions freely. *Who is the thirteenth guest?*"

"Marie Morgan!"

"I thought so," retorted Winston triumphantly. "Please give me the details of this strange bequest of Colonel Morgan's."

"He came to me about a month before his death, gave me a copy of his will and a sealed envelope. He told me of his plans for this birthday dinner to which his relatives were to be invited and of the announcement he intended to make then—that a large share of his estate was to be bequeathed to the thirteenth guest of the dinner, who was to be absent. He gave me no inkling as to the identity of this mysterious person but said the envelope, which I

was to open at a certain time, would give me the proper
information. He seemed to consider this dinner and the
strange bequest a good joke on his relatives; and informed
me that his attorney, Austin Barksdale, had been given the
same instructions as I had, so that if anything happened
to either of us the other could carry out the provisions of
the will.

"The appointed time came seme two months ago. I
opened the envelope and found only a sheet of paper with
the name Marie Morgan written on it. I wrote Miss Morgan at once and directed her to return to Ricksburg immediately as I had important news for her. She arrived three
or four days ago but I had not seen her for years and I
demanded positive identification, the letter I had written
her, before turning over the estate. She couldn't produce
it but said she would send for it. Day before yesterday
she telephoned me, saying that she could positively prove
her identity and requested me to meet her here late that
night. I consented but later became suspicious and did not
come."

"You had three visitors this afternoon, Mr. Thornton,
Miss Morgan's aunt and two men. What did they want?"

The banker stared at the district attorney's evident
knowledge of affairs which he felt were known only to
himself.

"Mrs. Grant wanted to know if I had seen her niece.
Mr. Adams said he knew the time had come for the trans-
fer to the thirteenth guest and demanded a share of the
estate."

"On what grounds?"

"That he is a half-brother of the late Colonel Morgan. He claims that the gold mines from which Morgan
made his money were an estate which belonged to all the
heirs of their mother and not to Morgan alone, that the
latter swindled the other heirs out of their shares before

they knew of the existence of the estate and later held the property in such a way that they were unable to gain their interests legally. He offered to show proof of his charges. But I told him I could do nothing for him. The third man said his name was Arthur Preston. He claimed to represent Miss Morgan and demanded that I carry out the provisions of the will immediately. I told him I would as soon as I had positive proof of her identity."

"This last man was the man called Tony who comprised one of the team that tortured you today to make you talk." It was not a question but a statement of fact.

"Yes."

"Very well. Now, here's another point: The girl who was murdered in this house night before last was Marie Morgan. The body is at Osterman's Mortuary. Who will this wealth go to now?"

"Her heirs."

Winston whirled on young Morgan.

"What heirs did your sister have?"

"Only me, so far as I know."

"Then you are the one who will gain enormously by her death?"

"Yes. But you're not insinuating—" The young man's eyes flashed dangerously and his fists clenched.

"No. Just making a plain statement of fact. Now—" Winston gasped as a thought struck him. In sudden alarm he looked at his watch. Two minutes before twelve! That last note had appointed the hour of twelve. "I must get back to the library at once!" he exclaimed breathlessly. "You come with me, Mr. Thornton. Morgan, you and the two officers go down to the treasure room and guard it with your lives. Don't hesitate to shoot to kill if you have to!"

Trembling with anticipation, he helped the old banker to his feet, and hurried him out of the tower into Colonel

Morgan's bedroom and toward the broad stairway beyond. He expected the next five minutes to be the crucial point of the whole mysterious affair.

24

The Zero Hour

District Attorney Winston's reappearance safe and sound brought evident relief to Grump and Sherwood. It showed in their faces.

"I've been worried about you," admitted the detective, mopping his perspiring forehead. "Those damn' phantom footsteps have been playin' a regular tune. I was afraid they'd got you."

"Not a chance," smiled Winston. "That was me making all the fuss."

"You? Then you found a way into the tower?"

"I did. And that isn't all I found. I discovered a room at the bottom of it containing millions of dollars in gold ingots. And in another room I found Murphy and Harrison and Mr. Thornton."

"Alive?" demanded Grump breathlessly.

"Yes—and kicking. I've brought Mr. Thornton back down here with me to prove it."

"It's all quite true," affirmed the banker, entering the room from the dark hall.

"God! It's worse'n a fairy story!" exclaimed Grump in bewilderment.

"I've found out a lot of things since I left," said Winston hurriedly. "But I haven't time to tell you about them now. That dark man, Preston, and Jensen have gone into town for a truck to haul away the gold so we'll probably see them soon. In the meantime, it's twelve o'clock, the time appointed in that last note for Marie's appearance. So be absolutely quiet and we'll see what happens. The zero hour is at hand."

The flashlights were extinguished and all four men lapsed into silence. Not even their breathing could be heard. Winston was holding his revolver ready for instant action and he felt sure that Grump was doing the same. The intense blackness with the complete silence and the uncertainty in all their minds as to what might happen within the next few moments create a suspense that was painful. Somebody cleared his throat noisily and there were quick, nervous little sounds as the others started.

"Is District Attorney Winston here?"

From somewhere in the darkness came the voice, a clear feminine voice a trifle breathless. Winston felt his heart hammering furiously. He had closed the door. He was positive that it had not opened. Nor had he heard any other noise. Yet there was that voice!

"Yes," he answered, making a tremendous effort to keep his voice evenly calm. "This is District Attorney Winston speaking."

"Are you alone?"

"No. Some of my men are with me."

"Very well. Have you a light?"

In answer he depressed the button of his flashlight and the beam cut through the darkness like a knife, revealing a figure standing across the room near the bookshelves. Winston gasped, for to all appearances it was the apparition which he twice had pursued up the stairs to the second floor. Following his lead, Grump's light now was assisting in dispelling the gloom and he heard amazed grunts from the other men present. He was furious to find that in spite of all his efforts at calmness his knees were trembling a bit. This figure was the exact counterpart of the corpse which he had found in that very room two nights before and which he knew positively was now in the embalming room of Osterman's Mortuary. The girl strode swiftly toward him but without a sound. Then he saw that she was wearing rubber-soled sport shoes.

"I am Marie Morgan," she said simply and extended her hand.

"M-Marie Morgan," he stammered as he hesitantly forced himself to take her hand.

"Yes." Her tone raised a little and she frowned as if slightly provoked at his strange actions. "Whom did you expect?"

"I didn't know," he confessed, then smiled feebly. "I've had so many strange occurrences to contend with the past two days that my nerves are a little shaken, I guess. But I'm here in answer to your note. What can I do for you?"

"I need your help," she answered quickly. "There is a plot against my life. That poor girl who was murdered here night before last was killed only because the murderers thought it was me they were strangling." She sobbed hysterically. "I've been so terrified the past two months that I haven't known which way to turn."

"Suppose you tell me the whole story," suggested Winston kindly. "I shall be glad to do all I can for you. But be as brief as possible, please."

He was expecting the return of Preston and Jensen any moment and he wished to have all possible facts in his possession before confronting them.

"My father, the late Colonel Morgan, left a very strange will," she continued. "Trust funds were provided for my mother, my brother and myself. But the estate was much smaller than we had been led to expect. The house and all its contents were bequeathed to a mysterious person who was not named in the will—to the absent thirteenth guest at his fatal birthday dinner. It said the person in question would be communicated with at the proper time. We waited anxiously to see who would get the old place but it remained vacant, still a part of the estate. For years we wondered who it had been left to but finally, with the passing of time, we gradually almost forgot about it.

"About two months ago in Paris I received letters from Mr. Thornton, the banker who was executor of the estate, and from Austin Barksdale, the attorney who drew up the will, requesting me to return to Ricksburg at once as they had important business to transact with me. This was within two weeks following my twenty-first birthday and I wondered if I was the thirteenth guest, if my father had left me the place to be given me at the age of twenty-one.

"I returned to the United States as soon as possible and immediately found myself the target of some gang. An attempt was made to murder me in New York where I received threatening letters saying I would be killed if I came on to Ricksburg. But I came on West by a roundabout way, attempting to keep in hiding. Yet they followed me. They almost got me in Chicago and I hurried on out here. I was afraid to go to a hotel so came directly to this old house to stay, feeling that I could hide here better than anywhere else. But someone had been here ahead of me. There were plenty of provisions in the kitchen and the telephone was connected. I telephoned Mr. Barksdale and Mr. Thornton, telling them who I was and asking them what they wanted with me. They laughed at me, saying that Marie Morgan was already in Ricksburg and that I was an impostor.

"I didn't know what to do but I realized that I must have help so I wrote those urgent notes to you and finally telephoned you late that night. I remained hidden in this house, even though I knew other people were in it because I remembered a lot of strange nooks and crannies in it which a stranger would never find.

"When I crept downstairs night before last to keep my appointment with you I found another girl who looked enough like me to be my twin sister lying on the floor of this room murdered. I screamed, locked the front door and rushed upstairs again to my hiding place on the third floor. When people approached where I was, I hid in the folding bed. And I've been afraid to move from there until today when the house finally quieted down so that I knew no one else was in it. Then I sent you another note. And here I am."

"H'm!" mused Winston. "A strange story indeed! Did you tell anyone in Europe the purpose of the trip before you left?"

"Yes. Prince Ratzpfund."

"Oh! Have you seen him since your arrival in America?"

"No."

"Did you have a plastic surgery operation performed on your face about two months ago in Chicago?"

"Of course not. How utterly ridiculous!"

"Have you visited your aunt, Mrs. Grant, since you arrived over here on this trip?"

"No. I was afraid to. This gang knew so much about my movements that I knew they would be looking for me there."

Winston swung his light around until it shone full in the face of Doctor Sherwood who was staring at the girl in open-mouthed stupefaction.

"Do you recognize this man?"

"No. I never saw him before."

"H'm! . . . You say you can give positive proof of your identity?"

"Absolutely. If you'll come up to the third floor with me I can show you all sorts of papers, including the letters from Mr. Thornton and Mr. Barksdale."

"Do you remember the wording of those letters?"

"Yes."

"Very well. This gentleman here is Mr. Thornton. Repeat the letter which he wrote you and see if he recognizes it."

Quickly the young woman recited several sentences. The old banker pondered a moment then nodded his head in approbation.

"I believe that's it, word for word," he responded.

"Then I'll take your word about your identity," said Winston. "But it might interest you to know that the girl who was murdered here night before last has been positively identified as you by your brother."

"My brother!" almost screamed the girl. "Is he here?"

"Yes. He's in the tower."

"The tower?"

"Yes. Don't you remember that round projection on the corner of this house? Well, it's hollow, with three rooms and a circular iron stairway connecting them. The bottom one contains many wooden packing cases filled with gold ingots, millions of dollars, and all a part of your legacy. Your brother, with two policemen, is down there now guarding what he thought was to be his."

"Well, he'd guard it just the same if he knew it wasn't," she retorted spiritedly.

With startling suddenness came the muffled sound of a shot. Winston rushed across the room and put his ear to the wall. Then came more shots.

"Morgan and the policemen evidently are attacked," he snapped. "The enemy must be in the tower. If we go in from that second-floor entrance—the only one we know of—we'll have them between two fires and their capture will just be a matter of time."

He rushed out of the library with Grump close behind, Thornton, Sherwood and the girl staring after them in stunned amazement.

They reached the second floor, heels pounding a stir-
ring tattoo, and Winston rushed into the former bedroom
of Colonel Morgan, his flashlight exploring a path ahead
for him. As he crossed the threshold, something struck
his left wrist a tremendous blow and his paralyzed fingers
allowed the light to drop to the floor, where it crashed
into oblivion. At the same instant someone leaped upon
him from behind. He stumbled and went down. Before he
could catch his breath, horribly powerful fingers were at
his throat, attempting to strangle him.

25

The Strangler

Winston was dazed by the suddenness and the almost complete success of the attack. Nearby, he could hear threshing sounds and heavy grunts indicative of Grump also struggling with an assailant. But he dared not divert his attention from his own plight. He realized that if he were to save his life he must bring to bear all the concentration and strength he possessed.

He was flat on his back now and the unknown was astride his chest. Powerful hands were at his throat and two awful thumbs were closing relentlessly against his windpipe. Then came sudden horrible realization. This must be the strangler at his throat, the man who had murdered that mysterious girl in the library and who had murdered Attorney Barksdale, the strangler who accomplished his awful purpose with such deadly certainty. Could he escape?

His gun was gone, knocked from his hand as he went down at the first unexpected onslaught. He had no idea where it was. In the intense darkness he could not even gain the slightest conception of his assailant. His hands went out, feeling over the floor for the gun. But the welcome coldness of its metal did not meet his exploring fingers. If he were to save himself, it must be by physical force.

Frantically he attempted to dislodge those horrible hands from about his throat. But his own hands and arms, strong as they were, accomplished nothing. Already his quick, gasping breaths were rattling in his constricted throat while his head whirled and pounded disconcertingly. And his efforts seemed merely to weaken him. He wondered, with a sudden flash of awful premonition, if this was to be his end. He realized that only a moment or two of consciousness was left him unless he did something immediately. And with renewed frenzy he fought for his life.

Quickly he lifted his legs, as if trying to touch his head with his toes. They brushed against something. He made another effort, a striving, that made his muscles creak and that shot sharp pains through them. But his legs now were in front of the strangler's face. He could feel them resting against something unyielding. It must be the man's head. Quickly he hooked his feet together then pushed with all his strength.

The sudden attack from such an unexpected quarter caught the man unawares. Thrown violently backward he was compelled to relinquish his grip but not before, it seemed to Winston, the powerful hands were to tear his head from his shoulders. But at last his throat was free.

The realization flowed through him like strong drink. He took half a dozen long, deep breaths, then followed up his temporary advantages. With their positions reversed he soon had his assailant at his mercy. Then he became aware of another figure groping about near him. Was he to be compelled to face still another attack?

"Grump?" he demanded anxiously.

"Yes," came the detective's welcome voice.

"Let's have a light."

The revealing beam of a flashlight cut through the darkness, centering on Winston and his captive.

"My God!" exclaimed the district attorney as he gazed down into the blinking eyes of his antagonist.

It was the heavy-set, sporty-looking man whom he had seen on the street in conversation with Dodge and the mysterious Jones.

"Who are you?" he demanded from his position atop the man's chest.

"J. S. Adams!" snapped the other, "a half-brother of the late Colonel Morgan, the damned old crook!"

Winston and Grump gazed at each other significantly. That voice, so very deep, and the name—Adams. This was the man who had phoned for Thornton the night of the murder. Was he the strangler? Together they hauled their captive to his feet and the detective snapped handcuffs on his thick, powerful wrists. To one side Winston could see another man stretched out on the floor. They took a look at him. He was of the gangster type, apparently one of the men who had been in the crowd the night that strange car had run Winston's machine into the ditch. Just now he was not in the least interested in the proceedings, his battered forehead giving the reason.

"I had to massage his head a little with my gun to make him behave," explained Grump grimly.

They both were anxious to question their prisoner but more important matters demanded attention at the moment. The big bed was swung to one side and the secret door which was the entrance to the treasure tower stood wide open. Winston hurried to it then retreated back into the room quickly as the firing stopped and a sudden rush of ascending feet sounded on the iron stairway. With flashlight and gun trained on the opening he waited. But not for long. The tower spat forth four men seemingly all at once. Winston recognized them all—Jensen, the dark man, Preston, and two more of the gangster type. The light seemed to stun them for a moment. They halted and stood blinking in its blinding glare.

"Throw up your hands, every one of you!" commanded Winston crisply. "I have you covered and I won't hesitate to kill if any of my orders are disobeyed. I'm not taking chances with this gang!"

There was a long pause. Winston cocked his revolver. In the tense silence the tiny click was unmistakable and abnormally loud. Jensen smiled sneeringly and raised his hands. The others followed suit. And in every right hand was a revolver.

"Ran out of cartridges, eh?" commented Winston. "I thought so when I heard the retreat start."

"Yes," admitted Jensen. "I can't see you beyond that damned light but I presume you're District Attorney Winston. It looks like you've got us!"

"Rather!" agreed Winston with grim humor. "It's really too bad, though, that you can't take the Morgan gold with you."

There was another rush of feet on the stairs, then young Morgan and the two policemen rushed into the room from the tower and the gang was completely cornered. Quickly they were disarmed and bound. A carefully guarded trip to the library followed. Then with all the principals in the mysterious drama gathered about him under the weird glow of the many candles in the big chandelier District Attorney Winston opened the final scene.

"I have enough on everyone of you to put you away for a long time," he began deliberately. "But before doing so, I wish to have all the details of this strange affair cleared up." He turned on Jensen. "You are the so-called Prince Ratzpfund." It wasn't a question but a statement of fact. Marie Morgan had already identified the man.

"Yes," admitted the handsome blonde crook.

"And you," turning to the tall dark man, "are the Arthur Preston who is called Tony." That, too, was a statement of fact for Doctor Sherwood had identified the man.

The accused refused to speak but his sullen glower in the district attorney's direction was answer enough.

"It's quite plain now," Winston continued with a calmness he did not feel. "A gang of international crooks, one of them posing as a Prince, discovers that an American girl is going to come into a rather mysterious piece of property. They have another girl made over by a plastic surgery operation to resemble her, then bring the bogus heiress here to claim the estate, confident that others of the gang will accomplish the death of the real Marie Morgan before she reaches Ricksburg.

"But their plans slip a little—the banker refusing to turn over the property without more positive identification of the girl than the gang is able to provide. The real Marie arrives and in attempting to murder her in this house they make a mistake and murder their own girl who is the decoy. Then, realizing that they must take desperate measures, they did the rest of the things which have kept us puzzled and on the jump the last two days, culminating in the kidnapping of Banker Thornton, from whom they secured information which enabled them to gain admittance to the tower, where they found the treasure.

"The only thing I don't know positively is the absolute identity of the actual murderer, although I presume it's you, Adams, because you tried to murder me in the same way that the bogus Marie Morgan and Attorney Barksdale were disposed of."

"It was," confessed J. S. Adams in his distinctive deep bass voice. "I murdered old Morgan, too, the night of that dinner by putting poison in his glass. The old devil stole the fortune for himself that belonged to all of us. After he had taken the gold out of the mines he was afraid to go to some big city to live. He knew I was on his trail. So he came here. At last he gave that dinner to mock us, his poor relatives, thinking that the hope of being remembered in his will would make us let him alone. But I knew that none of us would ever see a dollar of that money. And I murdered him. I intended to murder the whole family one at a time so that finally we would have to get what was coming to us, what he had stolen from us. But they escaped me. I'll get 'em all yet, though, I'll murder everybody by the name of Morgan until—"

He whirled and made a sudden mad rush at Marie, lifted his manacled hands high to strike her down. But Winston had been watching him with intense interest and a growing conviction that the man was mad. And he was prepared for some untoward act on the man's part. He lunged forward, seizing the man's coat collar, and hauled him back into the loving embrace of Murphy and Harrison.

"That fellow's as crazy as a loon!" volunteered the erstwhile Prince Ratzpfund. "We found him around here when we arrived and put up with him because he might be able to do us some good. And he did give us a few valuable pointers. But he committed those two murders without orders. We were as surprised at them as you were."

There were sudden footsteps in the dark hall beyond the library. Winston whirled and explored with his flashlight, his revolver ready for instant action, then gasped as he recognized two men advancing toward him—Dodge, the reporter, and his mysterious friend Jones. They blinked under the sudden glare but came forward resolutely with a provoking air of calm assurance. Jones paused in the doorway and surveyed the group within the library then smiled triumphantly and extended his hand toward the astounded Winston.

"Congratulations, Mr. Winston!" he exclaimed heartily. "You've done a nice night's work here, I must say."

"And who are you, may I ask?" demanded the district attorney, Dodge's conduct still rankling within him.

"George T. Appleton, federal agent," retorted the other and, throwing back his coat, exhibited the attractive badge of an agent of the Department of Justice, sometimes erroneously known as the "Secret Service."

"I've been following this gang of international crooks for a long, long time. Everyone of them is wanted for a long list of major offenses, both here and abroad."

"Then perhaps you can identify that man," pointing to 'Jensen.'

The officer laughed scornfully.

"I'll say I can!" he gloated. "He's known by half a hundred different names and titles in various parts of the world. A cleverer crook never breathed."

"Then he isn't Thor Jensen of Jensen and Jensen, New York, antique dealers?"

"He is Thor Jensen. But that firm has always been merely a cloak for the operations of the gang."

"Do you know this man here?" indicating Adams.

"I've talked with him here in town but he isn't a crook that I know of. Who is he?"

"A half-brother of old Colonel Morgan. He claims that the Morgan fortune rightfully belonged to the whole family and not to the old man alone, that the Colonel swindled the rest of the family out of their share. He's utterly crazy now, from brooding about the matter, I suppose. . . . Well, that's that. I guess there's nothing more we can do here."

Murphy and Harrison were armed and established as guards over the enormous treasure in the tower until a relief could be sent out from town, and the others prepared to depart. In some strange way, Marie Morgan was the only person left without means of transportation when District Attorney Winston started to his roadster. So he asked her to ride with him. A man simply had to be courteous.

"Tell me," he said as they sped along, "why you asked me to help you instead of writing to the police?"

"Because I'd seen your picture in the Ricksburg papers and somehow you looked so kind and helpful." She sighed and her head touched his shoulder.

"Well, I'm just twice as kind and helpful as I look," he retorted joyously and wondered how Hallud would accept a mistress.

And in direct violation of a law which he himself had sponsored, he drove the rest of the way with one hand.

ABOUT THE AUTHOR

Maurice Coons (July 18, 1902 - October 10, 1930) wrote under the pseudonym Armitage Trail. While he is best known for his 1930 novel, *Scarface,* it was preceded by this 1929 mystery, *The Thirteenth Guest,* and a couple dozen short stories (both detective fiction and gangster fiction) in *The Underworld Magazine, Detective Tales,* and other pulp magazines. Coons' gangster material was informed by his socializing with Chicago gangsters in the 1920s. When Howard Hughes bought the rights to *Scarface* (adapted into the 1932 film), Coons moved to Los Angeles. Coons did not adapt well to fame and fortune, as alcoholism and luxurious living quickly took a toll—he died of a heart attack at age 28. After Coons' death, *The Thirteenth Guest* was adapted, very loosely, to film twice, in 1932 (starring Ginger Rogers) and 1943 (with Helen Parrish).

COACHWHIP PUBLICATIONS
ALSO AVAILABLE

SCHOLAR TURNS DETECTIVE
IN TWO SOPHISTICATED MYSTERIES

MURDER IN THE ZOO
MURDER IN CHURCH

Babette Hughes

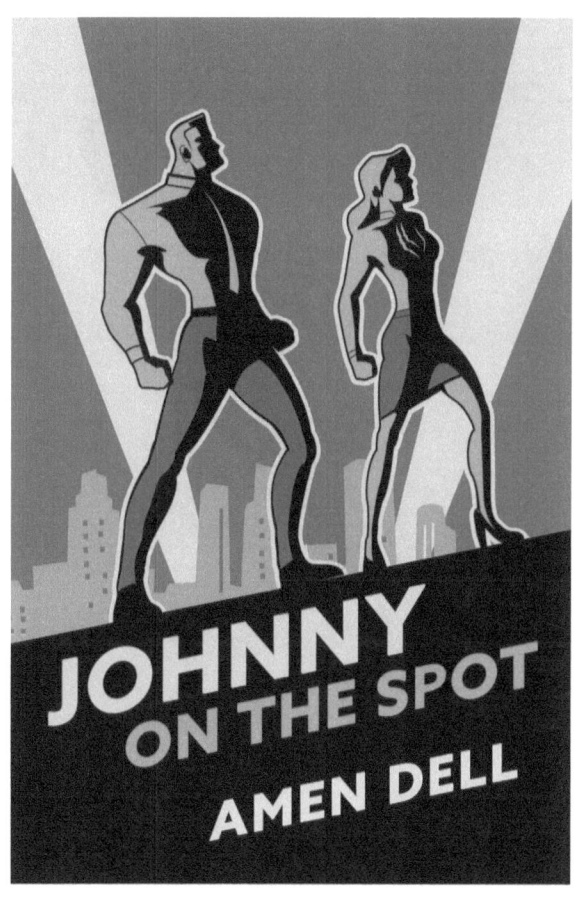

COACHWHIP PUBLICATIONS
ALSO AVAILABLE

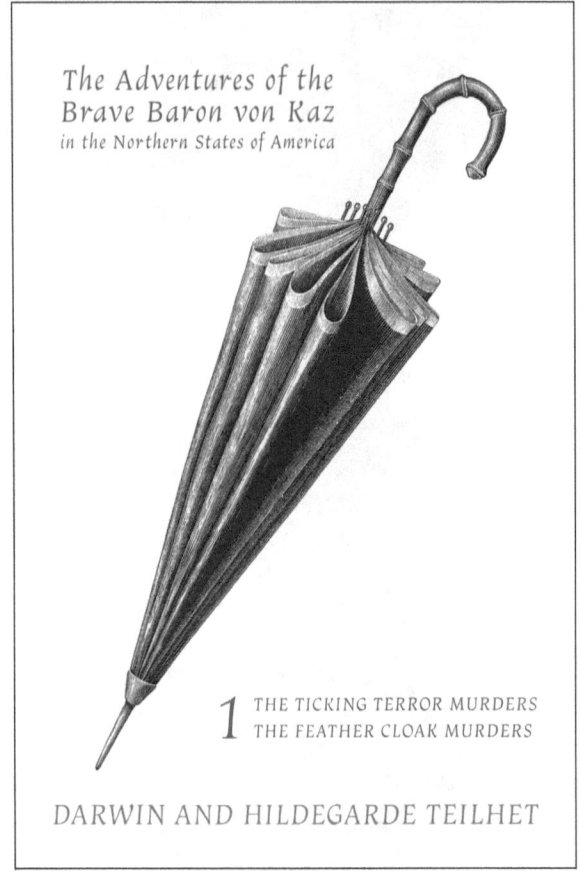

The Adventures of the
Brave Baron von Kaz
in the Northern States of America

1 THE TICKING TERROR MURDERS
  THE FEATHER CLOAK MURDERS

DARWIN AND HILDEGARDE TEILHET

COACHWHIPBOOKS.COM (PRINT)
COACHWHIP.COM (EPUB)

COACHWHIPBOOKS.COM (PRINT)

COACHWHIP.COM (EPUB)

Death Has
Seven Faces

HUGH AUSTIN

COACHWHIP PUBLICATIONS
ALSO AVAILABLE

The Black Gardenia
Elliot Paul

COACHWHIPBOOKS.COM (PRINT)
COACHWHIP.COM (EPUB)

PATTERN
IN BLACK
AND RED

FARADAY KEENE